The Grey Lady of Monarch Cove

WHITE RAVEN SERIES BOOK 4

AnneMarie Dapp

For the firefighters of the world.
Special thanks to the writing duo, Amber Anthony. Your support is priceless.

"The boundaries which divide Life from Death are at best shadowy and vague. Who shall say where the one ends, and where the other begins?"

— EDGAR ALLAN POE

Prologue

AIDAN AND JADE READIED THEMSELVES FOR THE LONG DAY AHEAD OF THEM. The newlyweds met their friends on the steps of the Scottish castle beneath charcoal grey skies. The staff waited in line to say their goodbyes. The storm had tapered off, with a light dusting of fog kissing the sea. Dougal, the Scottish Terrier, followed at Jade's heels, while Aidan carried Morrigan the White Raven's cage. They loaded themselves into two cars and arrived at the landing strip surrounded by fields of purple heather. Once the private jet was loaded, the group took their seats inside. Mrs. Macleary offered Champagne to the guests before takeoff. They sat back, readying themselves for the twelve-hour flight.

"Hopefully, we will have a smoother ride than last time," Jade said. Mary and Katie exchanged glances.

"Don't worry. We'll be fine," Jade said. For the next several hours, the group enjoyed their flight by catching up, eating, drinking, and sleeping. Before they realized, they were back in California. They said their goodbyes, promising to get together soon. After their driver dropped them off in Pacific Grove, Jade and Aidan took turns carrying their luggage and pets to the cottage.

"I'm dying for a hot shower," Jade said with a deep yawn.

"Good idea, love. Why don't you get started, and I'll get Dougal and Morrigan's supper ready?"

By the time she left the warmth of the bath, Aidan had lit a fire and fed the pets. Jade headed to the kitchen, but turned suddenly when she heard Dougal growling beneath the fireplace. She joined her husband in the living room. In disbelief, the couple stared at the portrait above the hearth.

"Oh, my God, Aidan."

The lone man, who once stood by the sea, had vanished. In his place was a grey lady surrounded by a shroud of monarch butterflies.

"What does it mean?" Jade asked.

"Seems like we have another mystery to solve," Aidan said.

Jade pushed a golden curl from her forehead and yawned. "Looks like it's time to get back to work. I guess our vacation's over."

"Don't worry." Aidan smiled down at her. "I promise we will unravel it. It's not the first time we've had a mystery to solve, and it may not be our last. But for now, let's go to bed. We will figure out everything in the morning."

Jade sighed, gazing into her husband's aquamarine eyes. "Hmm, that does sound nice."

He lifted her in his arms, carrying her to the bedroom. Gently, he laid her down atop the quilts, kissing her soft lips. Outside, the storm pounded the sandy beach, and lightning lit up the bedroom windows. Aidan moved Jade against his eager body, and they created their own rumblings beneath the satin sheets.

Chapter One

*H*ER CHESTNUT CURLS SWEPT ACROSS HER IVORY SHOULDERS AS SHE DIPPED *the paintbrush. She studied the unfinished portrait with reverence as her delicate hand moved gracefully over the blank canvas. The silver sheen of her Edwardian gown rippled with each dainty movement. The doorbell rang, and a dark-haired gentleman waited anxiously outside the mahogany door. Reluctantly, the young woman placed her wet brush on the palette and moved toward the parlor. The lady's husband and servants were away for the evening and the unexpected privacy brought a flush to her high cheekbones.*

For a moment, she stood in the doorway, twisting her wedding ring, trying to decide. Expectantly, she opened the door to gaze into her lover's hopeful brown eyes. Biting her lower lip, she moved backward with half-closed lids.

From the upstairs studio, an ebony cat circled the abandoned easel with purpose. When the old tom heard footsteps on the stairs, he leapt onto the pallet of fresh paint. Soft laughter floated down the hallway like tiny bells. The curious feline startled at the sound of the slamming door and knocked the unattended pallet to the floor. As the frightened pet rushed from the studio, he left behind a row of crimson paw prints in the fading light.

JADE SNUGGLED AGAINST HER HUSBAND'S CHEST, STEEL-GREY EYES fluttering open as he wrapped his protective arms around her.

"There's my lovely bride," Aidan said, lowering his lips to hers. "How did ye sleep, lass?"

"Hmm, good," she said, sitting up and stretching. "It's wonderful to be back home, but it seems strange to have to make my own coffee. I miss Mrs. Flannery already."

"Well, you stay warm in bed," he said, looking toward the window. "It's raining again. Don't want you to catch a chill. I'll make ye a cuppa."

Jade watched her husband's nude form disappear around the corner. After slipping on a robe from his suitcase, Aidan made his way into the modest kitchen.

She'd never tire of his perfect body and gorgeous face. And that was just his human side. The fact he was part selkie added another layer of enchantment. The day he'd transformed into a half-human seal hybrid was forever etched in her mind. During the metamorphosis, his lower body became sleek and powerful, unbelievably exotic and unearthly. After she'd witnessed his transformation, Aidan feared the truth would keep them apart. Yet, his hybrid nature undoubtably saved her from drowning, and she would always love him for it. Despite his brawny physique, her husband's hands were gentle as silk. Every touch stirred her passion, sending jolts of unimaginable sensations throughout her body. She sighed, reminiscing on their passionate evening the night before. The storm invigorated the newly-weds, electrifying their lovemaking.

"Looks like Mary stocked the kitchen up with groceries," Aidan called from the kitchen.

Jade reluctantly turned her thoughts to her morning routine and pulled her silk robe over a pearly white satin camise. A few minutes later, she joined her husband by the counter and wrapped her slender arms around his powerful hips.

"Aww, that's why she's my best friend. After taking care of the antique shop, she still makes time to ensure we're comfortable," Jade said.

Aidan nodded. "There's a note pinned to the fridge," he said, eyeing the delicate handwriting.

He grinned. "Mary says she wants us to rest up. Also mentions there's going to be a big storm passing through the next few days."

"Oh? Looks like we escaped the weather in Scotland, only to have it follow us home," Jade said with a yawn.

"It sure does." Aidan smiled down at his wife, admiring the soft glow of her cheeks in the morning light. "I'll be heading into work tomorrow, so we should snuggle up today and enjoy the fire."

"Sounds like a good idea, love. I'm still a bit jet lagged."

Jade pulled the belt of her satin robe tight and padded toward the fireplace. She let out her breath, enjoying the warmth of the flames. A strong wind whipped the sides of the cottage and a light spray of rain sluiced down the lace-covered windows.

"Thanks for adding wood to the fire." Jade's eyes rose to the portrait above the mantel, and she grimaced.

"Oh, God. I'd almost forgotten."

Aidan looked over his shoulder, frowning.

"What's wrong, love?"

"The painting is completely transformed. Our Scottish laird has been replaced by an Edwardian lady surrounded by monarch butterflies. Oddly, the entire painting has taken on a grey, misty appearance. I was hoping it was just a bad dream."

Joining Jade by the fireplace, Aidan encircled his large hands around his wife's petite waist. As his lips touched the delicate spot by the nape of her neck, she trembled with pleasure. Within moments, her anxiety melted beneath her husband's loving touch.

"Yes, I noticed this morning, darlin'. Appears the crazy portrait is back to its old tricks. I wonder what happened to the Scottish lad on the beach?"

Jade shrugged and shook her head. For a moment, the couple stood in silence, gazing up at the lady in grey.

When Aidan overheard Jade's stomach rumble, he took her hand and led her toward the dining room table. Once she took her seat, he hurried to the kitchen. As he stirred bell peppers and tofu into a sizzling frying pan, he glanced toward his wife. Realizing what she desired first thing in the morning, he set the pan to the side and set a mug of piping hot coffee on the table. Grateful for his thoughtfulness, she smiled up into her husband's adoring eyes.

"Thank you. You know how to make a girl happy," Jade said, blowing away the rising steam.

"You're welcome, lass. Don't worry. We have plenty of time to figure things out. Just relax this morning, and let me take care of you today."

Jade watched her husband make his way around the kitchen and smiled. She loved how natural everything settled despite their short time together.

Carrying two porcelain plates on his arm, he set them down on the dining room table.

"I bet you're famished after our lovely evening last night," he said with a wink.

Jade felt herself blush beneath her husband's aquamarine gaze. "Yes, I'm starving," she said, her breath hitching. "You gave me a workout, Laird MacFie. I'm looking forward to a possible encore tonight?"

Aidan chuckled, his hand moving over his wife's shoulder, then down her side.

"Maybe we won't have to wait until this evening," he said with a hint of a smile.

"Promises, promises," Jade answered, steel-grey eyes gleaming in the morning light.

"Aye, I always make good on my word, lass. Just make sure to finish your plate so ye have plenty of energy for the rest of the day."

Jade laughed as Dougal padded toward his bowl, stubby tale wiggling in delight.

Aidan took his seat across from his wife and took a sip of coffee. As the rain pounded onto the tin roof, Jade leaned back with a sigh. Their cottage by the sea was everything she'd ever dreamed of and more. Sometimes she felt like pinching herself just to make certain she wasn't dreaming.

"It's lovely having you across from me this morning, darling. You mentioned earlier we should make the cottage our main home?" Jade asked.

Aidan reached across the table and covered Jade's small hand in his own. "Aye. Seems like the perfect place. We can continue our runs on the beach and the horses will arrive in a few weeks once the barn's repairs are finished."

"I really love the idea. Can you imagine riding Blackjack and Bonnie along the shore? It will be a dream come true! But are you sure you won't miss your penthouse? It's so grand in comparison to the cottage."

"Well, I was thinking we could use the penthouse as our second home. Maybe we can go back and forth between the two? Also, you're welcome to store any of your antiques ye don't have space for. There's plenty of room."

Jade smiled. "Thank you, Aidan. You're always so thoughtful. And I was hoping you might prefer using the cottage as our primary residence. Honestly, the first time you spent the night it seemed so natural. I'm thrilled you feel at home here. There's such a deep connection to my ancestors within these walls. And since the Mackenzie's and MacFie's were friends years ago, it seems fitting that you're part of my family's legacy."

"Yes, it's incredible our clans knew each other over a century and a half ago. Appears we were destined to be together, love. And I feel the same way about the cottage. It seemed like home since the first night. Thankfully, we can finally put the Hunters' chapter behind us once and for all. Uncle Brodie promised to keep an eye out in Tobermory, but it sounds like most of the cult members were arrested during the Great Selkie Birthing."

"Thank God. Now we just need to solve the mystery of this portrait," Jade said, pushing a locket of sandy-blonde hair from her forehead. Placing her napkin by her plate, she left the table and moved toward the canvas above the fireplace. Aidan followed her to the living room.

"I don't really know what to think of the recent changes. On one hand, the painting has been a valuable tool. It provided a mirror into the past, and simultaneously warned us about future dangers. And now I realize the alterations were supplying clues all along. But so many questions remain. Why was the portrait in my shop to begin with? Where did it come from? Who's the artist?" Jade shook her head. "I think I'd feel better once I understand its true purpose. Mary and Katie's research was helpful regarding its connection to selkie lore. But the imagery has changed, and the Scottish laird vanished. Who's the mysterious lady in grey? I guess I'll have to start all over again." Folding her arms across her chest, she stepped closer to the portrait.

"Any fresh ideas this morning, love?" Aidan asked, staring at the mysterious canvas.

"From my art history background, I can assume a few basic facts. For one, the subject is wearing an embellished tea gown, which suggests the canvas represents a woman living near the turn of the twentieth century. If I had to hazard a guess, I'd say the imagery likely dates to the Edwardian period between 1901 to 1910. Happen to love the style. Many paintings from the era depict charming golden age scenes. A common theme portrays ladies of leisure enjoying afternoon tea parties. Dressed in flowing vintage gowns, the subjects lounge about, seemingly without a worry in the world.

Although, I must say, this painting gives off a strange melancholy feeling. The subject's grey dress matches the dark skies of the canvas. The seascape looks wild and untamed, even a bit threatening. Reminds me of some of the darker elements of the Romanticism Movement during the early to mid-nineteenth century, especially relating to elements of emotion and the power of nature. It's quite interesting considering the blending of styles. It gives me a jumping off point in my research. I believe it's time I put what I learned from my master's in art history to use. I was so preoccupied with getting the antique store off the ground and trying to figure out the strange happenings by the beach, I leaned on my friends for help. Now that the shop's stable, I think I'm going to put my degree to work."

"One of the many things I love about you," Aidan said, stroking her rosy cheek with the back of his hand. "You're as brilliant as you are bonnie." With a lopsided smile, he gazed at his wife in the firelit room.

Jade felt herself flush at the intensity in her husband's vibrant eyes. He moved her against his chest, kissing the top of her head.

"God, I cherish ye. Just let me know if I can help in any way."

An unexpected boom of thunder caused Morrigan the White Raven to fly from her perch toward the kitchen. She landed on top of the lace-covered windowsill and stretched her powerful wings in a fan of ivory feathers. The room darkened as storm clouds passed over the cottage.

"Are you ready for breakfast, my lady?" Jade asked.

Morrigan cawed in anticipation, bouncing her snowy head up and down, pale blue eyes flickering in the dim light.

Grinning, Jade moved toward the refrigerator and opened it. Inside, she noticed a large bowl of mash stored in a Tupperware next to a carton of almond milk. "Mary thought of everything. Not only did she stock the fridge, but she also made sure Morrigan would have breakfast when we arrived home from the wedding."

After spooning a generous portion of mash into her pet's bowl by the window, Jade pushed aside the lace curtain above the farmhouse sink. Torrents of rain pounded across white dunes, and frothy tides churned.

Sighing, she turned to her husband who had returned to his seat at the dining room table.

Jade joined him and took a sip of her coffee.

"I think this is going to be a day to stay inside by the fireplace. I just need a good book and…" Jade stopped mid-sentence as Aidan reached for her hand, sending ripples of pleasure over her skin. Will his touch always take my breath away? she wondered, imagining it would.

After breakfast, Jade brought their dishes to the sink. While the water ran over the porcelain plates, her husband moved closer, gently parting her sandy-blonde waves to the side while kissing the nape of her neck. A myriad of sensations rocked her body as his warm breath sent shivers down her spine.

"Are you ye sure you'll be reading all day, lass? I had a few other ideas in mind," Aidan said, his voice deepening as he drew her close.

"Mmm, you have no idea what your touch does to me, Laird MacFie."

Jade closed her eyes as her husband's lips warmed her skin."

"Aye, I feel the same. Glad we enjoyed a hearty breakfast. Since we're staying inside, I believe we are going to need all the energy we can muster."

Jade let out her breath, overwhelmed by their reality. They could finally enjoy some down time and concentrate on their domestic life.

Chapter Two

MADAME GARNIER AWOKE TO HER USUAL FLARE OF ARTHRITIC PAIN. Reluctantly, she climbed out of bed and made her way to the kitchen to prepare a pot of tea and take her pain medications. The recent storm managed to set her joints on fire. Her ebony cats, over a dozen now, moved between her spindly legs, crying plaintively for their breakfast. She enjoyed each one with loving devotion. Being they were all rescued from a nearby shelter, she'd become well-acquainted with the staff. A few of their employees enjoyed monthly palm readings at her modest cottage. Madame Garnier kept an eye out for the strays left behind. In return for her generosity, the ebony felines provided glimpses into the spirit realm. For long ago, she learned cats belonged to both sides of the veil. They were conduits between the living world and often accompanied and protected their mistress between the planes of the deceased. Yes, she enjoyed her familiars with her heart and soul, and they reciprocated their appreciation in turn.

As she was lost in thought, the tea kettle shrieked its welcoming call. She filled the antique pot with a generous portion of herbal tea. Afterward, she prepared her pets' bowls before gingerly sitting down at the kitchen table and lighting a kerosene lamp. Amber light flickered over the black embroidered tablecloth, illuminating her deck of Tarot cards. Her ebony eyes flickered with curiosity.

Although her aging body was troubling her this stormy morning, she was on a mission. She'd enjoyed helping her friends at the antique shop the past few weeks. Being around precious heirlooms invoked memories of her youth. The psychic sensed many things, but last evening's dream was particularly troubling. She'd perceived a misty grey woman dressed in Edwardian garb. This was not unusual. It wasn't the first time she'd had visions of the mysterious lady. However, this prescience had an urgency to it. And she suspected something darker lingering in the atmosphere compared to the previous premonitions. She closed her eyes, feeling a light tingling sensation on the back of her neck.

Her eldest cat, Pyewacket, jumped onto her lap, his emerald eyes glowing in the soft light.

"My sweet boy. Do you sense it, too? You always snuggle close when a spirit is nearby. Shall we find our answers, then?" she asked the old feline while he stared into her ebony eyes, speaking without words. Listening to his deep purring lulled her into a meditative state.

Yes, the other side wants my attention today, she thought, sensing the veil's membrane thinning while time slipped away. Oh, yes, the spirits were awake, and they had plenty to say. They often whispered, and if ignored, they would eventually scream. What was their intention? She wasn't entirely sure. But she knew with proper reflection, the universe would provide clarity. After her second cup of tea, she shuffled her Tarot deck, looking for answers. She was not disappointed.

Chapter Three

AFTER A SENSUAL DAY AND NIGHT FILLED WITH DOMESTIC BLISS, THE newlyweds realized it was time to get back to work. Jade took Morrigan and Dougal to the truck before saying goodbye to her handsome husband. Aidan stood on the whitewashed porch with his coffee cup, the early morning sun reflecting his vivid blue eyes.

"You call me if anything comes up, darlin'. I hate to be away for the next couple of days, but that's a fireman's schedule."

Jade rushed back to the front steps, wrapping her slender arms around him. "Knew your job was hectic when I married you, Laird MacFie. I'll miss you, love. Be safe."

"Will do," Aidan said, pulling his wife close against his powerful body. He kissed her passionately, while she melted into his embrace. Once she was behind the wheel, Jade waved goodbye from the driver's seat. She watched Aidan in the review mirror, standing on the porch with a soft smile as she made her way down the driveway.

Her body quivered where his hands lingered, and she tried her best to focus on the day ahead.

There were plenty of projects to tackle since she'd been away from the antique shop. After stopping by her favorite coffee drive-through, she headed to work. As she sipped a warm mocha, her mind wandered to the tasks of the day. As much as she missed Aidan, she was eager to be back to the store. New shipments of merchandise had arrived earlier in the week according to Mary's note. Despite the many hours of preparation ahead, she looked forward to experiencing her first holiday season in Pacific Grove.

Turning the radio to a popular Christmas music station, Jade headed downtown. While she hummed along to *Jingle Bell Rock*, she admired an abundance of Christmas wreaths and cheerful decorations adorning the festive streets. She loved the old-fashioned holiday vibe, and her mind was abuzz with inspiration.

Once she parked the truck, she grabbed Dougal's leash and Morrigan's cage and hurried to the front door of Antiquities and Novelties of Pacific Grove. She breathed in the familiar scent of potpourri and mulberry candles. Boxes were stacked near the register, the latest inventory ready to be organized. After setting up the pets, she moved to her desk. A note taped to the top of the antique register.

Hey, girl,
    A new shipment arrived the night before I left for Scotland. Hope you enjoy your new merchandise. Looking forward to my next visit.
    Love ya bunches,
    Mary.

P. S. Paul sends his love. We're meeting for dinner in a couple weeks at his parents' house. Yikes! Things are getting serious. Double date for New Year's Eve? I think so! I'll call you when it gets closer!

Jade smiled reading the note. She was thrilled her best friend discovered true love. Even better that her boyfriend was buddies with Aidan. After all, Sheriff Paul Rheinstein saved her husband's life during the Hunters' kidnapping ordeal. She'd forever be in his debt. Yes, they would enjoy many double dates in the future. With just under an hour before the shop opened, she popped in her favorite Nat King Cole Christmas CD into the stereo. If she focused, there would be just enough time to catalog the new merchandise before her attention was divided between customers and decorating.

Her mind raced with ideas as she took a sip of coffee. While she hunted for a utility knife to open the cardboard boxes stacked by her desk, the room darkened. A clap of thunder hinted the possibility of another storm.

Once she'd moved a shipment container onto her worktable, she began sorting the new arrivals. She checked off her packing slip, noting each antique. A collection of old-fashioned Christmas collectibles and ornaments were set inside the first box. In her notebook, she sketched out her plans for their placement. After organizing the pieces, she went to work on a shipment of Victorian-era tea pots. These she arranged inside a glass case by the front entrance. By the time she'd opened the third carton, she was almost finished with her mocha. Dougal trotted over, wagging his stubby tail in anticipation of a potty break. She bent down, giving her pup a pat on the head.

"Ready for a walk, boy? I could use another coffee myself. Give me just a second and we'll go." The terrier yipped in excitement, seeming to understand.

When the box opener sliced through the taped cardboard box, her eyes widened. On closer inspection, the container appeared empty, minus a stack of vintage envelopes and cards yellowed with age. Thumbing through them, she realized they were Christmas Eve invitations. Blinking in surprise, she noted the date of the party, December 24th, 1906. Dougal whined and circled her feet as she held the tarnished paper in the fading light.

"Incredible," she whispered to herself. "Hey, buddy, it looks like we received something special in this order. These invitations date back to the year of the San Francisco 1906 earthquake. Imagine!" she said, smiling down at the anxious dog.

Dougal plopped down onto his belly, laying his wiry chin on her Ked sneakers and sighed.

"Says, it's for a Christmas Eve ball and portrait reveal. Hosted by the O'Shea's. I have no idea who they are, but the invitation sounds lovely."

Jade studied the card with interest, reading the opening line of fine calligraphy.

"You are solicited to attend the Grand Christmas Eve Ball and Portrait Unveiling of Lady Deidre O'Shea."

Dougal's pointy ears twitched while he released an impatient moan.

"It's all right, buddy. Just let me look through this box and we can go for a potty break. Sound good?"

The Scottish terrier's ebony eyes searched Jade's face, and he rolled on his side.

"Good boy. This should only take a minute. Promise."

After the pup relaxed, Jade thumbed through the rest of the invitations inside the box. At first it appeared the remaining contents were simple duplicates. Yet, once she reached the bottom of the carton, she uncovered a rectangular item covered in tissue paper. After pushing the fragile wrapping aside, a flash of tarnished silver twinkled in the hazy light. When she lifted the object closer, a light scent of jasmine lingered. The vintage photograph, protected by a pewter frame, caught her by surprise. She chewed her bottom lip, trying to remember where she'd ordered it. Dougal whimpered by her feet as she studied the photo.

"What's wrong, boy?" Jade knelt and scratched behind his pointy ears before turning her attention back to the image. Taking a sip of cold coffee, she leaned forward and examined the image of a young woman reclining daintily on her wicker chair atop a cheery white porch facing the sea. Petite gloved hands folded neatly on her lap as she gazed toward the tides.

Two men were off to the side, standing beneath a pitched doorway. The older gentleman appeared in his late thirties to early forties, wearing a three-piece suit which buttoned to the neckline with small lapel and tie. His companion wore a less formal attire—corduroy pants, and vest, along with a tweed flat cap. While the mysterious woman gazed toward the sea with a demure smile, the men focused on the young lady, seemingly mesmerized by her elegant appearance. Bright eyes, high cheekbones, and a rosebud mouth framed by dark ringlets complimenting an angelic face. An hour-glass figure contained beautifully within layers of silk and damask. The seemingly romantic photograph appeared strangely familiar, leaving Jade experiencing a combination of intrigue and slight apprehensiveness. Although the woman offered a soft smile, her sorrowful eyes told another story.

From her extensive knowledge of art history, she assumed the image represented the Edwardian period. It was evident by the flowing gown, delicately folded at the skirt, while curving inward at her tiny waist, before flaring out near the hemline. The soft, fluttery style reminded Jade of warm summer days sipping tea by the seashore. Not being able to pinpoint the source of her unease, the image summoned a combination of curiosity and dread. After examining the photograph from different angles, she carefully re-wrapped the mysterious antique back inside the faded tissue paper. Slipping the treasure into her purse, she decided to re-visit the image at home. For now, it would not go up for sale.

After Jade snapped a leash on Dougal, they made their way over to a large cypress at the end of the block. Before heading back to the shop, she headed to her favorite café and ordered a large mocha, along with a farmers' market salad to go. The business was pet friendly, so she was able to bring Dougal inside. The terrier sniffed the cement floor with interest, searching for leftover crumbs and other tasty treats. The barista, a teenage boy with a shock of dyed blue hair, offered the terrier a dog biscuit from behind the counter. The happy pup carried the coveted treat back to the antique store, his stubby tail wiggling the entire way. Rain slipped through the storm clouds, pelting them sharply as they made their way down the empty sidewalk. With the jingle of the bell, Morrigan cawed a greeting from her perch.

"We're back, sweetie; I'll share my salad with you. Would you like that, beautiful girl?"

The raven flapped her pearly feathers in the muted light, eyeing her mistress with pale blue eyes. Before setting out lunch, Jade thumbed through Dougal's bag of food and treats behind her register. Having already devoured his treat from the café, he was ready for seconds. The terrier sat on his haunches, stubby tail thrumming in anticipation.

Jade handed him a rawhide chew which he politely took, his fuzzy beard tickling the tips of her fingers. She laughed, watching him trot to his bed by the desk, plopping down with his back feet straddled behind him. Once Dougal was distracted by his favorite afternoon snack, she forked out a portion of her salad into Morrigan's bowl before eating her own meal by the register. Watching the rain trickle over the front window, she relaxed in her chair, enjoying the sound of low thunder rumbling overhead.

Monday trailed by slowly. The storm allowed Jade to focus on organizing the new arrivals. Each passing holiday provided an opportunity to update the theme of the shop. Realizing Christmas season was on the horizon, she focused on making the store as festive as possible.

After sorting through a carton of vintage books, she discovered one of her favorites, Charles Dickens' *Christmas Carol*. Beaming, she opened the cover. Between the tarnished pages of fine literature were a collection of exquisite-colored illustrations. She inhaled the lingering scent of vanilla and stale coffee as her mind raced with possibilities. Along with being an uplifting story, the classic tale offered spooky undertones. Halloween was her favorite holiday, Christmas being a close second. It had taken some searching, but she'd managed to acquire a first edition copy of Dickens' classic. Now she had the perfect jumping off place for December's theme. She'd coordinate many of the new antique arrivals and the vintage treasures in the front window.

With her mind brimming with ideas, Jade jotted down a list in her notebook, making sure to schedule some Christmas tree shopping. A potted evergreen would be perfect for displaying her assortment of heirloom ornaments.

Holding her breath, she imagined her first Christmas with Aidan. Would they finally be able to put the past behind them? Were her dreams coming true? She felt hopeful as her day flew by peacefully.

Shortly before closing the shop, Madame Garnier entered with a jingle of a bell above her silver head. Both Jade and Morrigan turned their attention to the elderly woman. Dougal trotted over from his bed by the window, tongue hanging out in excitement. The psychic stroked the terrier's muzzle with her ebony glove before turning her full attention to Jade.

"Good afternoon, Mrs. MacFie!" She reached out her bony arms toward Jade and gave her a hug. Black lace covered her from her collar to the hem of her Victorian-styled gown. Jade had been surprised by her vintage attire the first time they met. However, she'd grown accustomed to the psychic's eccentricities, even looking forward to them.

"Congratulations are in order, mademoiselle. Must say you are simply glowing!" She cocked her head to the side and smiled. "Ah, and I see your aura is a lovely green today. That's your heart Chakra shining. Love is in the air!"

Madame Garnier folded her gloved hands together, focusing on Jade's wedding band.

"Thank you, Madame Garnier! It's wonderful to see you. I've been meaning to call you and thank you for your help at the shop. Mary said you were incredible with the customers. We wouldn't have been able to finish everything we needed in Scotland without your assistance. And I have a check for you! Let me fetch it from the register."

Jade moved toward the counter and tapped the steel buttons atop the vintage machine. With the tickle of an antique bell, the bronze cash drawer popped open with a groan to its hinges. She reached toward the back tray to retrieve a plain white envelope with the words, *Madame Garnier*.

"Oh, that's exceedingly kind. But it was my pleasure," the elderly woman said, shaking her head when Jade offered the envelope with a smile.

"No need for payment. Please, put your money away. I'll just pick out a little something before I leave. Working at your store was wonderful for an old soul like me." She pushed back a silver-colored curl peeking out from beneath her lacy bonnet.

"Oh, but you must be paid for your hard work. I simply won't take no for an answer," Jade said with a smile.

Madame Garnier glanced about the room before walking toward an oak table embellished with green Depression glasses. The corners of her mouth lifted when she noticed the set of Jadeite goblets and matching pitcher. A sliver of sunlight slipped from the front window, highlighting the sparkling collection.

"Perhaps I might take home this set for volunteering at the shop? I've always had a fondness for Jadeite glassware. The color reminds me of Pyewacket's gorgeous green eyes. Yes, indeed," she mused, staring off in space.

"Pyewacket?"

"Don't you remember, mademoiselle? You met him the day of your first Tarot reading. He's my oldest and dearest companion. Yes, we've shared several lifetimes together," she reminisced, with a dreamy look in her eyes.

"Oh, I know which cat you're talking about. He was sitting at my feet during my Tarot card reading. If I recall, his eyes were an exquisite shade of green." A small smile flickered as she studied Madame Garnier in the soft light. "I'm curious, did you happen to choose the name Pyewacket from the movie, *Bell, Book, and Candle*?"

"Aww! You're a clever girl. I most certainly did!"

Jade grinned, thinking back to her mother and their love of film noir.

"Adore that story. Mom and I must have watched it a dozen times over the years. I always liked the idea of having a…" Jade trailed off trying to remember the correct word.

"Familiar." The elderly woman finished her sentence.

"Yes, that's it."

Madame Garnier's ebony eyes sparkled. "Why, dear, haven't you realized you already have a familiar?" she asked, glancing at Morrigan.

Jade's mouth dropped open. "My raven?"

Madame Garnier chuckled, moving closer to the ivory corvid.

"Well, of course. Why there is no doubt. Just look at the way she follows your every move," the elderly woman said, focused on the bird's pale blue eyes. "And I understand this lovely creature assisted in finding your husband during his imprisonment near the Pacific Grove Monarch Sanctuary. Mary explained your bird showed up at the abandoned house nearby."

Jade studied her beloved pet, heart racing. "Yes, and I dreamed about Morrigan appearing at the exact hideout the night before."

Madame Garnier folded her laced-covered hands together.

"Of course, dear. That's how the connection develops with our animal companions. Mary explained how she and Deputy Rheinstein followed your raven to the beach near your cottage. Morrigan led them to the exact location you were being held prisoner. Your raven's a powerful guide, and it's evident your souls crossed before. In fact, it wouldn't surprise me if you've known your handsome husband in a previous incarnation."

"That's a wild thought," Jade said, trying to let it all sink in.

Hoping to change the subject, Jade placed the white envelope into the psychic's gloved hands.

"Thank you, dear. It appears you won't take no for an answer," Madame Garnier said, eyeing the amount of the check. "My, you're more than generous."

"Of course. And please take the Jadeite set as well," she said, turning toward the table of colorful heirlooms.

The elderly woman's silver eyebrows rose in surprise.

"Really, I insist. I truly can't thank you enough for helping Mary at the shop. It allowed Aidan and I to discover the underlying cause of our rather…unusual business in Scotland."

Madame Garnier nodded, patting the back of Jade's left hand. After admiring the glistening sapphire and diamond wedding ring sparkling in the dim light, she sighed.

"Oh, dear. Isn't it lovely! When the pads of her gloved fingers grazed the top of the jeweled surface, her smile faltered.

"This ring has quite an unusual history, doesn't it? An heirloom of the most unique circumstances. Imagine much transpired during your visit abroad," the psychic said, lips pursing together.

Jade nodded. She wondered if she'd ever get used to Madame Garnier's psychic gifts.

"Yes, my wedding ring originally belonged to Aidan's great-grand-mother. Dates to the eighteenth century. In fact, it's been passed down through many generations."

"Yes, I feel that it's been a valued treasure for the MacFie Clan. Now it's your turn to bring it into the twenty-first century. Love to hear more about your findings in Scotland. As you can imagine, things have a way of changing quickly around here. Has everything been alright since you've arrived home?"

Jade's smile slowly faded. "Well, that's the thing. Do you remember when I told you about the mysterious portrait at my cottage? The one with the Scottish laird gazing toward the sea?"

"Of course, I remember. The painting has a connection to the other side. After all, the canvas offered clues during Aidan's disappearance."

"Yes, it most certainly did. According to Mary, the image changed back to its original form when we were in Scotland. However, when we arrived home…there were alterations," Jade said.

"Really? Well, I'm not surprised."

Jade's stomach tightened. "I'm not sure I follow, Madame Garnier?" she said, sensing she was not going to like the answer.

The elderly woman moved toward Morrigan's perch, eyeing the raven with curiosity. Gently, she ran a gloved finger across the raven's pearly cheek before turning her attention to Jade.

"You see, I've sensed something was a little off this morning. Just to be sure, I visited my Tarot cards. As I suspected, they had plenty to say." The psychic tsked and shook her head.

"Oh?" Jade held her breath, fearing the worst. As desperate as she was for life to return to normal, the portrait's alterations suggested otherwise.

Madame Garnier studied Jade in the fading light. "Mademoiselle, I don't want to frighten you. That is never my intention. Maybe if I start at the beginning everything will make sense. That way, we can ready ourselves for any unusual happenings. It's always best to be prepared in these kinds of situations."

"Not sure I quite follow. Do you think Aidan and I are still in danger? We believed things were calming down once we returned from our trip."

Madame Garnier offered a tight smile.

"I'm glad things are settling, but try not to become too complacent just yet. Maybe I can shine some light."

Jade feigned a smile, feeling apprehensive. She steeled herself, trying to keep an open mind.

"Yes, please. Love to hear more about your findings."

"Excellent. We'll start at the beginning; and prepare. Rest assured; everything will fall into place."

"Would you like a seat?" Jade asked, pointing toward a nineteenth century Regency table she'd been using to organize the new arrivals.

"That would be lovely," Madame Garnier said, moving toward the mahogany antique.

"Perfect. Let me just clear some space so you can be comfortable. May I get you something to drink before we start? Have some iced tea in the fridge, or I can make a pot of coffee."

"Well, iced tea sounds lovely, dear, but don't trouble yourself at my expense."

Jade smiled, pulling out a velvet-backed chair for Madame Garnier.

"No trouble at all. Please make yourself comfortable."

Once she took a seat, Jade finished removing the cardboard boxes before fetching a glass of cold tea from a small fridge behind the register.

"Oh, thank you." The elderly woman took a sip; reflections of condensation glistened on the polished crystal.

When Jade joined her, she was met with Madame Garnier's intense gaze.

"Mademoiselle, do you remember the day I first visited your shop?"

"Of course, I do. It was the afternoon of my grand opening. I'm grateful you stopped by."

"As am I. You assumed it was mere coincidence that our paths crossed that day. But fate was most definitely involved. You should know our meeting was predestined."

"Oh?" Jade's eyebrows rose in curiosity.

"Well, you see, I was drawn to the antique store that afternoon. Honestly, I felt a pull the moment I passed by in my Cadillac. I was driving down Lighthouse Avenue on my way to pick up supper at the local café. And then I heard it."

"What did you hear?" Jade asked, steeling herself.

"It was a whisper of sorts." The psychic took another sip of tea and sat back in her chair. Nearly a minute stretched before Madame Garnier spoke again. Jade listened to the clinking of ice cubes hitting the side of the crystal glass. When the psychic-medium continued, her voice took on a wistful quality and her ebony eyes shone with purpose.

"I believe you've been in contact with the other side longer than you realize. Either in dreams, or while asleep, the veil responds to your spirit. You have the gift, mademoiselle. There is no doubt you're an empath, and I suspect, a conduit to the other side."

Jade shook her head, trying to understand. "Well, yes, and no. My premonitions commonly present as dreams. Other times it's just a hunch, like when I followed the monarch butterflies to the Hunters' hideout. Just a feeling, really."

Madame Garnier nodded, folding her gloved hands together. "Yes, it varies. Now, I didn't hear a voice that fateful day. More like a shadow of one. An echo, really. Well, anyway, I beckoned to make your acquaintance. And that's just what I did!"

"Interesting," Jade said, intrigued to learn more about Madame Garnier's psychic abilities.

"Of course, I've always adored antique shops. So many whispers from the past eager to be heard. And when I first noticed you behind the register, well, it was obvious to me you were special. You may remember me mentioning I sensed spirits around you?"

As she said this, Morrigan cawed from her perch, flashing ivory feathers in the muted December light.

Jade nodded, thinking back to that hazy October day. Little did she know her entire life would soon be turned upside down.

"Yes, to be honest your comments alarmed me. I wasn't sure what to make of it. But time passed, and I'm coming to accept that life is full of unexplained phenomenon. Are you still sensing a presence?" Jade asked.

Madame Garnier closed her eyes a moment, trying to gather her thoughts.

"Good question. Let me explain the best way I can. You see, sometimes spirits and energies are drawn to the living. And other times, they find solace in places they once knew. Spirit may attach to both. As you may have already guessed, certain locals are natural gathering stops for the undead. An antique shop is the perfect conduit for souls who have passed through the veil but are not ready to leave the world of the living. Something as simple as an antique ring or a favorite hairbrush may attract restless beings. Yes, I sensed it the minute I entered your store. There's a hot bed of activity brimming to the surface. Interestingly, it's not just the objects which attract the attention of the other side."

"Oh?" Jade raised her eyebrows in anticipation. "What else could it be, Madame Garnier?"

"Well, if you want the truth, it's you, dear."

Jade bit her bottom lip. "Me? But why? I don't understand."

"Yes, it must seem strange to wrap your head around the idea. After all, you're just coming into your power. It's quite impressive, really. I sensed your abilities when we first met. After your first Tarot reading, there was no doubt in my mind. Remember when I suggested your dreams were possible glimpses into the past and future?"

Jade nodded, resting her palms on the table. "I'll be forever grateful for your suggestion of listening to my dreams and believing my hunches. If I hadn't taken your advice, I don't believe I would have found Aidan and his kidnappers. Not sure how things would have turned out without your encouragement."

Madame Garnier smiled. "Such a blessing you escaped unharmed. So, once again, I implore you to embrace your unique attributes. Try not to shy away even if the visions seem overwhelming at times. With the right intention, your unique gift will open doors you never even imagined."

"Thank you for putting it that way. Makes it a little easier to digest. But I must be honest, these abilities can be overwhelming. Hoped everything would just go back to normal once we arrived home."

"Well, I was relieved to hear those terrible men were captured after their kidnapping attempt," the psychic said, crossing her arms over her narrow chest.

"Yes, and more members were arrested in Scotland. We discovered a whole hive of them. It's quite the story when you have time. But for now, high-ranking members of the cult are currently in jail, without bond, in Tobermory, Scotland. Thankfully, the Hunters' organization seems to be out of commission for the time being. It's quite the talk of the village right now according to Aidan's uncle."

"That's wonderful. Love to hear more about it. It's a relief knowing they're no longer a threat. And I imagine you want to get back to a normal life with your handsome husband," Madame Garnier said, gazing toward the hazy window.

"But what exactly is normal?" she asked, making air quotes with her gloved hands. "It seems to me that people seek to categorize everything into perfect little boxes. Anything outside their imagined perimeters is often considered abnormal. The idea doesn't sit well with me. Never has. As you already know, the world possesses eternally curious and beautiful forms. You're standing at the threshold of unlocking life's mysteries. With time and patience, your dreams and visions will illuminate this truth."

"It's just overwhelming sometimes," Jade said with a sigh. Dougal, sensing her anxiety trotted over and plopped himself down next to her Keds.

"What else is coming my way? I've already been kidnapped and escaped a blood-thirsty cult determined to wipe out an entire race of supernatural beings. Can't that be enough for now? Haven't I paid my dues? Honestly, I just want to settle down for a bit and enjoy a quiet life with Aidan."

"Of course, my dear. Peace and quiet have their rewards, but I'd like to pose a question to you. I don't expect for you to answer right away. Just consider it."

"Alright," Jade said, leaning forward.

"If someone was in great peril, and you had the means to help, would you?" Madame Garnier asked.

Jade chewed on her bottom lip and nodded. "If I could help someone in need, I'm sure I would. Never could stand the thought of anyone suffering."

"Of course, not. Sensed your lovely aura when we first met. It radiates kindness and empathy. Mademoiselle, I'm not the only one aware, however. Your energy is a beacon for those seeking assistance. Why, it's not a question of if they'll reach out to you, only a matter of when."

Jade was overwhelmed by the idea, but curious about the implications.

"It's funny you mention this now. I met a fascinating woman during my trip to Scotland. She suggested something quite similar. It's intriguing, but also scary. I really don't want to attract that kind of attention." She laughed, trying to make light of the idea.

Jade hesitated to mention the woman she was talking about was a selkie. Was Madame Garnier already aware of the existence of supernatural beings? she wondered.

"I realize it's a lot to take in. Your ancestors possessed the same gift, there's little doubt. It might be something to explore when you can find the time," Madame Garnier said.

Jade gulped, thinking back to her great-grandmother's diaries and the fact she experienced frequent visions along the Oregon and California Trails. Her dreams and foresight saved lives and helped heal her beloved fiancé.

"It's not a coincidence your love of antiques," Madame Garnier continued, setting her glass onto the coaster. Drops of condensation rolled down the side of the crystal heirloom. "I positively feel your connection to the past."

"Well, yes. Suppose antiquity has always been a subject of fascination. Since I was a young girl, I adored heirlooms and vintage collectibles. It's why I pursued a Master's in art history. Both my mother and grandmother were antique collectors."

"I'm not surprised. And were they...sensitive?"

"Funny you should ask. Grandmother was quite intuitive. She always knew when someone was about to visit or call. Really fascinating. She even predicted our next-door neighbor's passing one evening." Jade folded her hands beneath her chin, resting her elbows on the polished mahogany table. "I remember sitting in the dining room, listening to the hail hitting the bay window across from the table. Quite a storm that night. Halfway through supper, my gram casually mentioned Mr. Stevenson would soon be joining his wife. I just stared at her while she scooped up a forkful of mashed potatoes and continued eating. Her comment was so casual, like she was just discussing the weather. What made her statement so remarkable was the fact that our neighbor, Mr. Stevenson, lost his wife the previous year to advanced Alzheimer's. My mom tried to change the subject, but gram was insistent on the subject. Around midnight, just as I was dozing off to the sound of heavy rain, the scream of an ambulance jarred me from my sleep. When I looked out my window, there were paramedics and an ambulance next door. Poor Mr. Stevenson was taken away on a stretcher. I found out the next day he had suffered a double coronary and died on the way to the hospital.

"We sat at the breakfast table discussing the incident. Mother, being a devout Catholic, insisted grandmother's prediction was just a strange coincidence. Supernatural ideas were not something she would even consider. She wouldn't entertain any mention of the paranormal. Years later, my friends and I visited a local fair. After playing some carny games, and riding rollercoasters until we were dizzy, we noticed a rainbow-colored tent advertising a fortune teller. Holding our breaths, we peered inside. Within the glow of candlelight, an elderly woman studied a neon-colored crystal ball. With a silver scarf covering salt and pepper hair, she appeared positively mesmerized. After my girlfriends and I purchased our tickets, we waited in line, hoping to uncover details concerning our future love lives. But when it was my turn, my mother appeared out of nowhere and blocked the entrance. After a considerable time of pleading, and predictable teenage angst, my mom insisted I leave immediately or be grounded an entire month. To this day, I have no idea why she was there to begin with. Just remember being mortified being the only one left out."

"Interesting, mademoiselle. Well, I'm sure your mother was trying to protect you in her own way. Wouldn't be surprised if your grand-mère was gifted. The art of *seeing* passes down through the generations. And being you're from a Catholic background, the psychic gift may have made your mother uneasy. I've often had to hide my abilities from family members, so I know first-hand. My parents were devout Catholics themselves and feared my unusual abilities. Sadly, people sometimes confuse psychic abilities with the dark arts. This couldn't be further from the truth.

"It might be an interesting exercise to research the location of your antique shop. Dramatic events sometimes cause spirits to linger. Then again, your bartering of antiques raises my suspicions. Spirit can attach to certain objects, and the fact you are sensitive may put fuel to the fire. And as far as the portrait's concerned, I imagine there may be more than one answer. Perhaps a lost soul has attached itself and is simply unwilling to cross over. Then again, there is another explanation we haven't even considered." The psychic-medium locked eyes with her friend. "Have you ever entertained the notion your own abilities may be influencing the changes in the canvas?"

Jade sucked in her breath. "You...think the alterations are my doing?"

Madame Garnier touched the back of Jade's hand. "Well, yes, and no. It's possible the alterations in the portrait are manifestations of your psychic abilities. You can't deny that you've predicted things that have come to pass. As we discussed earlier, your dreams and visions led you to Aidan's kidnappers back in October. And then there's your love of antiques. It could very well be the previous owner was involved with the arts as well. Coincidence? Perhaps the painting is a simple conduit."

"Well, I'm not an artist by any stretch of the imagination. Seriously, I can't imagine having any influence on the painting. It must be something... or someone else."

"Maybe. Yet, I sense the alterations might be a combination of your sensitivity and a spirit reaching out from the other side. Art can manifest in ways you might not imagine."

Jade shook her head. "Hoped things would settle after our trip to Scotland. It feels like we're headed back to square one with this mystery."

Madame Garnier nodded with sympathy. "May I give you a bit of advice from an old woman who has seen her share of the world?"

Jade smiled. "Of course."

"The fact you are sensitive doesn't have to be a curse. It can be overwhelming. In fact, my psychic abilities surfaced at an early age. It was confusing and often terrifying when I was a child. You see, I always sensed spirits around me. Even departed family members made their presence known. My deceased grand-mère appeared in my bedroom shortly after her passing. It seems like only yesterday. If I remember correctly, I was saying my prayers when she appeared by my bed. Her face was so kind, her eyes full of love. We'd been close and seeing her again brought me such joy. To my delight, she continued to visit me over the years. Mother walked in on us one day when we were discussing my first day of high school. When I explained who I was talking to, she crossed herself and told me to never say such things. Whenever I broached the subject with my parents, they dismissed it as childhood fantasies. Eventually I kept my visions and feelings to myself, realizing talking about it only frightened my family. As a teenager, I began understanding my gift. It was empowering being able to open the door to the other side. If you think of it that way, the power of seeing is an opportunity. You may be able to help those in need when you're ready."

"How would I even begin to help someone?" Jade asked, her brows furrowing.

"That's an excellent question. Sometimes souls find themselves trapped between worlds. They don't realize they've left their mortal coil. Lost and confused, they often gravitate toward sensitive souls. Especially if their life ended unexpectedly or violently. They may be angry or confused. These are the souls that need the help of the living. Unable to cross over, the spirits are left in a state of limbo."

Jade shook her head. "That's a terrible thought. How frightening for the person trapped. If there is someone reaching out concerning the portrait, I need to find out how I can help them. Aidan and I were shocked when we came home from vacation. The painting completely changed. The Scottish laird has been replaced by a smoky figure of an Edwardian-styled woman."

Madame Garnier's brow raised.

"That is interesting. Wonder if I might see it sometime. Perhaps I'll get some insight."

"Oh, yes! Love for you to visit the cottage. In fact, if you'd like, it would be lovely to have you over for dinner this week."

"What a pleasure! I'd be honored," Madame Garnier said.

"Wonderful. Aidan will be home from work in a couple of days. Would Friday evening work for you?"

"Oh, yes. I'd enjoy that very much."

"Perfect. We could meet around 6:30 p.m.?"

"Works for me. I just need to feed my cats before I leave. May I bring something?"

"Just your wonderful company, Madame Garnier. Oh, and I wanted to share one more thing." Jade stood from her seat and headed toward the front desk. Searching between two cardboard boxes, she retrieved a canvas bag embroidered with the Scottish Flag.

"Picked up some gifts for you while on vacation. There's some candy and a few trinkets from the tourist shops in Tobermory. I even found a black cat mug! Hope you like it."

The elderly woman's eyes glistened with tears. "My, you are such a thoughtful young lady."

"Your help was priceless. Love to hire you again in the future if you're interested. I believe Aidan and I will be visiting Scotland quite a bit over the next few months. So, it's wonderful to have someone I can rely on while we're out of town."

The psychic gathered her purse and bag of souvenirs. "Pleasure. And it will be lovely dining with you and your handsome husband." Madame Garnier turned toward the front window with a grimace. "Feels like another storm is coming. Can feel it in my bones. Stay warm and safe, mademoiselle."

"You, too. Have a safe trip home."

Dougal followed the elderly woman to the door and watched her slowly cross the street to an ebony Cadillac.

After Madame Garnier drove away, Jade turned her open sign to closed and gathered her receipts for the day. Shaking her head, a smile moved over her face realizing the shop was making a nice profit since its opening. Before leaving, she grabbed her purse, suddenly remembering she'd forgotten to share the mysterious photograph during her visit. Being psychic, would Madame Garnier pick up energy from the vintage item? She'd make sure to ask her Friday night.

After locking up, Jade clipped on Dougal's leash and carried Morrigan's cage to the truck. With winter on the horizon, 6 p.m. was dark and chilly. Heavy mist covered the Ford pickup's windshield while they made their way down Lighthouse Avenue. A rumble of thunder boomed, and torrents of rain sluiced downward. With the wipers on high, she headed to Trader Joe's to stock up on fresh vegetables and dinner supplies. Once she parked, she told her pets she'd be right back. A gusty wind whipped the umbrella inside out before she reached the entrance to the market. Absently, she wiped the icy raindrops from her rosy cheeks and hurried inside. The narrow aisles, crowded with busy shoppers, made it a challenging excursion. After gathering her ingredients, she waited in line with her purchases. She noticed a family of four entering through the rain-streaked glass doors with umbrellas and soaked coats. Two young children raced toward the candy aisle while their parents followed in quick pursuit.

Dougal was peering out the window when she made her way back to the truck. His ebony paws swiped at the glass, eager for Jade's return.

"Hold on, buddy. Let me just get these groceries and we'll get you home." After tucking the bags in the backseat next to Morrigan's cage, Jade hurried back to the driver's side and turned on the ignition. She released her breath when the heater warmed the interior and leaned back against the seat.

With a deep yawn, she backed out of the parking space. Dougal curled up on Jade's lap, thumping his stubby tail. Stroking his ebony coat, they headed home to the sound of drumming rain. Glancing in the rearview mirror, Jade noticed Morrigan was fast asleep in her carrier. Her pale beak buried beneath a snowy wing.

While heavy winds battered the sides of the pickup, a siren jolted her from her daydreams. With the wipers on high, she pulled to the side of the road to let the ambulance pass. Before taking their exit, Jade noticed an old Fiat rolled on its side by the shoulder of the road. The back of the car smashed, while its emergency lights flashed in the gloomy haze. A paramedic was tending to the passenger, while a second wheeled a gurney. Jade blessed herself and said a silent prayer for the driver. It was a relief when they reached the cobblestone entrance to their cottage. The balmy aroma of the sea greeted her when she opened the driver's side door. Jade's golden tresses whipped against her flushed cheeks and prickled her grey eyes. Once her pets were comfortable inside, she fetched the bags of groceries.

Before making a fire, she clicked on the radio and hummed along to *The Little Drummer Boy*. Shivering, she searched for a comfortable set of flannel pajamas in the dresser, stepped into a pair of pink slippers, and padded over to the fireplace. When the flames danced in the cheery hearth, and the sweet scent of birchwood filled the cottage, she turned her attention to dinner. Her pets eagerly devoured their supper while she finished preparing her own evening meal. Listening to the gale bombard the whitewashed walls of the cottage, she sat at the kitchen table, enjoying a French bread bowl brimming with homemade broccoli soup. After dinner, she gathered ingredients for fresh cocoa. Slicing cubes of dark chocolate into a glass container, she warmed almond milk and cinnamon, stirring them together into an antique copper pan. If she was going to endure another tempest, she was determined to make the best of it. Before long, the savory scents mingled with the aroma of burning firewood, and she took a seat on the couch. Blowing the steam from her hot chocolate, she studied the Edwardian photograph. Dougal curled up next to her, sniffing the silver frame with curiosity. Jade chewed her bottom lip, noticing the terrier's pointy hackles.

"What's the matter, boy?"

The dog released a low growl before laying his muzzle onto Jade's lap. She scratched him between the ears, imagining the storm was making him nervous. Hail beat down onto the tin roof, while the lights flickered. Moments before losing power, Jade set the framed photo on the coffee table before heading into the kitchen to retrieve fresh candles. She'd made a habit to keep them in stock with the frequent power outages. While searching in the kitchen drawer, her skin prickled with goosebumps. A low buzzing reverberated throughout the cottage. Jade blinked, confused by the unfamiliar sound. Clutching the candles in her trembling hand, she returned to the fireplace to light the pewter candelabra. Just as she was bending down toward the hearth, the scent of jasmine filled the room.

Holding her breath, she stood from the spot. What she witnessed did not immediately register. In disbelief, she observed a misty form hovering near the dining room table. At first, it appeared translucent, expanding, and pulsating just yards away. Small particles of light flickered as the apparition slowly solidified. Without fully understanding why, Jade moved from the fireplace and began taking hesitant steps toward the strange phenomenon. As she drew closer, minute orbs merged into an upright figure of a young woman. The translucent specter floated down the hall, disappearing into the darkness.

Dougal jumped from the couch, darting toward the mysterious apparition. Tentatively, Jade carried the candelabra and followed. As she tried to summon her courage, the terrier released an anguished howl from the bedroom. With heart racing, she rushed toward the room. Between the bed and dresser, the unnerved dog cowered, hackles up and pointy ears flattened against his dark head. As she lowered herself next to the frightened pup, Jade immediately noticed a torn paper pinned beneath his paws. A vintage copy of *Wuthering Heights* had fallen to the floor, ripping a page from its binding. Not understanding, she placed the book back on the bedstand and focused on the terrier. Twisting up onto her lap, she hugged the pup tightly.

"What happened, buddy? Did the book fall on you?"

Whimpering, he hid his fuzzy muzzle beneath her arm. For several moments, they simply sat together on the floor, listening to the wind and rain.

Seeming to recover, Dougal trotted toward the bed and jumped on top of the quilted duvet. After setting the candelabra on the cherrywood table, Jade took a seat on the edge of the mattress. Holding the torn page beneath the flickering lamplight, she noticed a crimson-colored smear near the top paragraph, and she read the passage in disbelief.

"Only do not leave me in this abyss, where I cannot find you! It is unutterable!

I cannot live without my life! I cannot live without my soul!"

Wuthering Heights had been one of her favorite gothic novels since she was a teenager. She'd read the line before, but seeing it now chilled her to the bone. There was no obvious reason for the book to have fallen. She'd remembered placing it on the nightstand the evening before. As for a draft, the bedroom window was locked. Earthquake? Possible. But what about the mysterious figure? Am I seeing things? she wondered.

The sound of her buzzing cellphone snapped her back to reality. She took her candelabra with her to the dining room and answered.

"Hello, Aidan."

"Hello, darlin'. You sound out of breath; is everything all right?"

"Um, I think so. We lost power a little while ago. Dougal seems jumpy. There was a crash in the bedroom right before you called. When I went to check it out, one of my novels was lying on the ground. Did you feel an earthquake by chance?"

"I didn't, but I'll check online. You sound really spooked."

She took a seat at the dining room table. "It's probably nothing. Discovered an old vintage photograph of an Edwardian woman at the shop today. Quite lovely, but something about the image gave me the oddest feeling. Brought it back to the house. Strange, but I was studying the photograph when the lights went out. Then I saw something…unbelievable. I'm still trying to process everything."

"Did you make sure to set the alarm?" Aidan asked, his voice dripping with worry.

"Yes, everything's locked up," Jade said, trying her best to keep her voice steady.

"Good. What did you see?"

"It's difficult to explain, but I'll try. I really don't want you to worry."

"What's going on at the cottage?" Aidan asked.

Jade took a deep breath, trying her best to hide the tremor in her voice. "A few minutes ago, I heard a buzzing sound coming from the dining room. When I went to investigate, I noticed a misty haze by the table. There were prisms of light pulsing in the dark. Not quite sure how to describe it, but there appeared to be a bright halo of a woman. Before I realized it, I was following the glowing form into the bedroom, and that's when I heard the crash. When I looked to see what had fallen, Dougal was cowering in the corner. My copy of *Wuthering Heights* was on the ground, and one of the pages rested between his paws. Really bizarre. The good news is he's not hurt or anything. Just seems a bit uneasy."

Aidan was quiet on the other end, and Jade immediately wished she'd hadn't told him. The last thing he needed was to be distracted at work. Being a firefighter was serious business, and her husband needed to have his head in the game.

"I should come back to the cottage. I don't like the idea that you're dealing with this alone."

"Oh, no love. Shouldn't have even mentioned it. Probably just a bunch of silly coincidences with the storm and all. I don't know, maybe I imagined the woman. My eyes are probably playing tricks on me."

"Are you sure? What if it comes back?"

"Well, even if it does, I'm not sure you could do anything about it."

"You're a brave lass. Just wish I could be with you tonight. Promise me you'll keep your phone close and call me immediately if anything else happens."

"Will do. And please don't worry; we'll be fine. Just been a long day."

"I'm glad you told me, love. Don't ever feel the need to hold back anything. We're in this together. Counting the hours until I'm home with ye. Can't wait to hold you in my arms again."

Jade sighed. "Hmm, looking forward to it. Miss you so much. Please stay safe and don't worry about anything. Dougal's by my side, ready to protect me."

"Glad to hear it," Aidan said with a chuckle.

"Oh, before I forget, Madame Garnier visited the shop this afternoon, so I invited her to the cottage Friday night. Hope you don't mind. Figured she might have some ideas about the crazy phantom portrait. Maybe even some insight concerning tonight."

"Sounds wonderful. Looking forward to it. You just call me anytime if you're feeling spooked. Worry about you being by yourself at the cottage."

"Oh, I'm not alone. Dougal and Morrigan are taking wonderful care of me while you're away."

"Glad to hear it. Love ye. Have a good night's sleep," Aidan said.

"Good night. Love you."

Once Jade clicked off the phone, she took a deep breath and headed to the kitchen. Hearing her husband's reassuring words eased her weary mind. After washing her mug and giving Dougal a quick potty break, she readied herself for bed. She reached for her novel on the nightstand, then decided against it. As much as she loved the story, she'd had enough spooky excitement for one night.

Outside, the storm raged while she slipped into a dreamless sleep.

Chapter Four

THE NEXT FEW DAYS WERE A WHIRLWIND AT THE ANTIQUE SHOP. NEW orders arrived, and Jade spent her time unpacking merchandise and assisting customers. With the Christmas rush in full swing, she considered hiring extra staff. Despite her work overload, she was content knowing her business was profitable the first year. Her mind wandered while she sorted through box after box of antiques. She found herself daydreaming the hours away, relishing the fact she would be celebrating her first Christmas as a newlywed. She looked forward to receiving their special houseguest Friday evening. Perhaps Madame Garnier might shed light on the phantom portrait and the strange events at the cottage. While the skies darkened, she rubbed her arms as frigid air made its way beneath the door. With a lull in foot traffic, she concentrated on her new vintage ornaments and focused on transforming antiquities and novelties into a winter wonderland. If she focused, Jade would likely manage a festive Christmas Eve party for the shop. Just as she was breaking down the last of her shipping containers, she noticed a weathered newspaper inside a cardboard box.

Jade sucked in her breath, recognizing the mysterious lady in grey. In the fading light, she read the vintage wedding announcement.

The Carmel Times

February 14th, 1906
Deidre Doyle, Seamstress, Age 17, engaged to wealthy Bank Manager,
Thomas O'Shea, Age 38.

Shaking her head, she wondered why she hadn't noticed the newspaper article before.

Was it mixed in with the shipment of the vintage photograph and invitations? she wondered. Jade made it a habit to order merchandise from a variety of estate sales in the area. After her first Carmel purchase, several boxes shipped from a company called *Treasures in the Attic*. Although she distinctively remembered choosing a variety of beautiful 19th century teapots, vintage photographs and wedding invitations were not part of the order. Jade carefully placed the newspaper article into a manilla envelope before setting it into her purse. The announcement might tie into her research concerning the Edwardian photograph. Something bothered her about the image, but she couldn't put her finger on it. She'd mention it to Madame Garnier when she visited. After all, her friend had been a resident of Pacific Grove for over six decades, arriving from Paris in her late teens. *Was the psychic-medium aware of Carmel history?* she wondered. If the photograph came from the estate sale last summer, then perhaps she might find some answers in Carmel-by-the-Sea. From what she understood, the property was currently on the market.

Jade worked the remainder of the day with her mind preoccupied. By the time she arrived home, she was ready for bed. After a quick supper and cleanup, she drifted off to the sounds of the sea cresting the shore.

۞

B<small>ENEATH THE PROTECTION OF THE CHARCOAL-GREY AWNING, AN ANGEL-FACED</small>
woman descended the front porch steps of a gothic-styled estate. Absently
pushing a brunette ringlet beneath her broad silk summer bonnet, her
chiffon gown matched the cerulean sky. The lace accents of her bodice
flickered ever so softly in the breeze, while the aroma of jasmine kissed the
heady air. Her coachman escorted her to the four-wheel horse-drawn
carriage. Once inside, the young lady reclined against sage green velvet
cushions and moved a satin blanket across her lap. With a gentle flick of the

coachman's reins, the pair of ebony geldings made their way across the cobblestone streets. As they neared their destination, the scent of golden seas mingled with the warm summer breeze. Nearing Main Street, they parked across the white, sandy beach.

Assisted from the carriage, she turned to her driver with a bright smile.

"Thank you, Samuel. I'll be shopping until late this afternoon. Feel free to take your lunch. I'll be back by 4:00 p.m."

"Thank you, madame." He tilted his hat, watching her make her way toward the shops overlooking the azure Pacific Ocean. The young lady listened to the seagulls' cry as they dived toward the glassy waves. Her Edwardian gown fluttered as she casually made her way along the wooden-planked sidewalks. Gentlemen of varying ages tipped their hats as she gracefully passed, admiring her hourglass figure and refined appearance. She took her time shopping in the expensive boutiques and shops, purchasing whatever struck her fancy. After spending a quiet afternoon, she returned to her horses and buggy. It would not do to be late, if she were to be home to oversee dinner preparations. Her husband was a stickler for punctuality and loathed to wait. Her driver rushed to her side, taking her purchases so she would not have the chore of carrying them herself. She smiled as he placed her new hat boxes inside. Just as she was getting ready to leave, she turned toward the white sandy beach. A group of young men were congregating around a collection of easels and cooking pots.

"Samuel, please wait just a bit. I'd like to look at the artwork for a moment," she said, pointing a gloved hand toward the coastline.

"Of course, ma'am."

The wind whipped the sides of her chiffon gown as she made her way towards the seashore. Anxiously, she walked toward the artists. A tall gentleman with dark-brown hair smiled; his whiskey-colored eyes were flecked with gold, reflecting the vibrant hues of the azure sea. The corners of his mouth lifted while she hesitated on the wooden-planked sidewalk. With her mind made up, she crossed the distance between them, throwing caution to the wind.

❦

JADE AWOKE EARLY IN THE MORNING, GROGGY AND LIGHTHEADED. THE strange image of the mysterious woman by the beach haunted her waking hours. The following evening, the dream sequence repeated itself, once again ending with the Edwardian lady heading toward the seashore. By the end of the week, she had no doubt the grey lady was the demure woman from the vintage photograph.

Chapter Five

FRIDAY NIGHT STARTED OFF PLEASANTLY ENOUGH. AIDAN GREETED HIS WIFE at the door with a colorful bouquet, along with a crystal glass of chardonnay. She gathered up the collection of lilacs and roses, before throwing her arms around her husband's neck. Jade nestled against his broad chest breathing in his clean scent.

"Missed you, love," he murmured against her ear, his deep voice sending delightful shivers down her spine.

"So happy you're home," Jade responded.

Aidan gathered his wife into his powerful arms and carried her inside. Dougal followed close behind his master's heels, tongue hanging out the side of his mouth.

"Darlin', I started a fire. However, I must warn you…"

Jade's grin slowly disappeared as she looked up at the portrait above the fireplace.

"Yep. Figured you might need a glass of wine before seeing it. The figure appears to have moved again. Let me help settle the pets and we'll sort this out."

Leaving his wife by the fireplace with mouth agape, Aidan hurried over to the raven's traveling cage. Once the door was open, Morrigan took flight, landing on the back of the sofa behind her mistress. Baby blue eyes flashed, and the corvid released her high-pitched caw.

Jade gazed toward the portrait, arms crossed.

"Oh, dear God. The grey lady is moving!"

Aidan rushed to her side, speechless as the painted figure turned in real-time. In her left hand hung a leather satchel, while the right one grasped a kerosene lamp. In the distance, inky waves crashed along the cove.

For nearly five minutes, the couple watched breathlessly. When the movement finally ceased, Aidan turned to his wife.

"Lass, I've never seen anything like it before. Seems to have stopped for now. We figured it out last time; I'm sure we can do it again."

With a groan, Jade moved toward the kitchen. "I can't focus with Madame Garnier on her way. Let me get dinner started and maybe she'll have some insight after we eat."

"Good idea. Looking forward to receiving our first houseguest," Aidan said, before kissing Jade's flushed cheek.

As she collected ingredients for dinner, a flash of lightning streaked across the night sky. When she gazed out the window above the kitchen sink, the lights flickered.

"Wow, these storms have been constant since we arrived home. Hope Madame Garnier is safe driving over in this rain."

"She's an independent lady. I'd be more than happy to give her a ride, but something tells me she would politely refuse my offer," Aidan said with a grin.

"Agreed," Jade said as her phone beeped.

She retrieved her cellphone from the counter and read the text message.

"Looks like Madame Garnier is on her way but wants to finish a couple of errands before supper. Let me see if she'll take your offer." Jade typed a new message, hoping her friend might agree to be picked up.

Moments later, her phone beeped again. Jade shook her head. "You were right, darling. Says she's fine driving. A little rain never hurt anyone."

Aidan wrapped his hands around his wife's waist and nuzzled the back of her neck. Heat rose to her face as his breath warmed her skin. She let out a sigh, while chopping a bulb of garlic.

"Here, let me give you a hand," Aidan said, taking out a second cutting board from the cabinet.

Jade wiggled her nose as her husband serrated a yellow onion next to her.

"Had the feeling she'd decline," Aidan said with a smile.

"Yes, I figured," Jade said. She watched her husband make his way around the kitchen. "I can handle dinner if you want to rest a bit. Three days stretches at the fire department must be exhausting."

He chuckled. "Nothing I'm not used to, lass. Took a shower before you arrived home. So, I'm wide awake."

Jade turned toward him, raking his wavy hair back with her splayed fingers.

"Hmm, sorry to have missed that," she said with a wiggle of her eyebrows.

Aidan gave her bottom a firm pat before reaching for a green pepper.

"Looks like we'll have to take a raincheck after our guest leaves tonight."

Jade laughed. "Sounds lovely, Laird MacFie."

They talked about their day as they worked side-by-side in the modest kitchen. Soon the fresh scents of garlic and savory tomato sauce filled the cottage. By the time the couple finished making supper, the storm was raging. Dougal raced to the front door at the sound of soft tapping. Madame Garnier shivered beneath the shelter of the porch, holding a small fir tree wrapped in gold foil.

Aidan escorted the elderly woman inside while Jade hurried over to greet her.

"What weather! Goodness," Madame Garnier said, rubbing her gloved hands together. Pushing back silver locks from her forehead, she moved her lace shawl around her narrow shoulders and gazed around the room.

"Oh, what a lovely home. Brought you a little housewarming present. It's a fir. Picked it up at the nursery down the street from my home. With the holidays upon us, I thought you might enjoy planting the tree after Christmas. It's a tiny thing; might look nice on the dining table."

"Oh, it's lovely," Jade said, taking the pot in her arms and breathing in the fresh pine scent. "I have the perfect little ornaments for it, too. Thank you."

She carried the tree to the dining room while her husband took Madame Garnier's wool coat.

Aidan grinned down at the petite senior citizen. "Please make yourself comfortable. It's a pleasure to have your lovely company tonight. Jade just finished making pasta. May we offer you a glass of wine?"

"Oh, yes. Thank you," the psychic said, her dark eyes gleaming.

Aidan pulled out a seat for Madame Garnier before carrying her coat and purse to the closet.

"Red or white?" Jade asked, proffering two bottles.

"Red would be lovely."

Thunder rolled overhead as Dougal curled around the elderly woman's boots.

"Sounds like quite a storm," Aidan said, helping Jade finish the table with bowls of fresh pasta and salad, while Madame Garnier took a sip of Cabernet from her crystal glass.

"Oh, nothing like enjoying a winter storm inside with good friends."

Once the women were both seated, Aidan took his place at the head of the table. "You're our first official houseguest as a married couple. It's an honor to have you, Madame Garnier. Jade and I are forever grateful for your assistance with the Hunters. Your suggestion to listen to her instincts, and journal her dreams, really paid off. It undoubtably helped her uncover their secret lair."

"Well, that warms my heart, Aidan. Your beautiful wife is quite gifted. And from that delicious aroma, it appears she's a talented cook as well."

"Aww, thank you Madame Garnier. Aidan helped with dinner. Hubby's a genius in the kitchen. One of his many talents," Jade said.

Aidan smiled at the compliment, admiring his wife as soft candlelight danced along her golden curls.

"Wonderful. I'm just so pleased to join you tonight," Madame Garnier answered.

The rain pounded the tin roof as Aidan served a healthy portion of pasta onto Madame Garnier's plate. Jade passed the salad afterward. They were quiet as they helped themselves to dinner.

"Simply delicious!" Madame Garnier exclaimed, spooning up a forkful of spaghetti and washing it down with a sip of Cabernet.

"Must admit, I've fallen into quite the routine over the past few years. Spend most evenings with my lovely cats and sometimes dine alone at the café down the block on the weekends. This is such a lovely treat."

"Oh, the pleasure is ours," Aidan said, taking a sip of Cabernet. Dougal thumped his tail before resting his fuzzy muzzle on their guest's leather boots.

Madame Garnier forked a mouthful of salad and sat back in her chair. As she scanned the room, her smile faded. "I believe some unsolved mysteries await us," she said, turning toward Jade. "Your second sight is going to be important. There's an unusual energy in your lovely home."

Jade exchanged glances with Aidan. He took her hand in his and gave it a light squeeze, sensing his wife's uncertainty.

"I was afraid you might sense something unusual. But I'm glad you mentioned it. Perhaps after dinner I might show you some items from the shop? There's a vintage photo, party invitations, and a 1906 wedding announcement which recently came into my possession. And perhaps you can take a closer look at the portrait above the fireplace? Love to have your thoughts," Jade said, before taking a sip of chardonnay.

"Yes, I felt some heavy energy when I entered your home. It's a charming cottage, but it appears you're not alone."

Jade shuddered at her words. "Worried you might say something like that. There's been some strange activity at the house since we came back from vacation."

Madame Garnier nodded, turning her attention to Aidan. "Young man, I sensed a presence around your beautiful wife when we first met."

"Yes, I remember her mentioning it. Honestly, your warning unnerved her at the time."

"Sorry. We talked about this at the antique shop earlier in the week. My intention was not to frighten her. You see, it was obvious Jade was special the moment we were introduced. And of course, after our Tarot session, I knew for certain. She's sensitive to the other side. Imagine your wife's been this way her entire life. Just didn't realize her gifts. Simple things like knowing who's calling before answering the phone. Or sensing people's intentions. These are all signs of psychic abilities. Dreaming of events before they happen is a strong indicator as well."

Jade nodded. "Yes, I've always experienced unusual dreams and premonitions. Before I met Aidan, I'd just chalk it up to my imagination. I never realized my visions could be so powerful."

Madame Garnier reached for Jade's hand and smiled. "Yes, you're beginning to trust your gift. And you may soon learn spirits sense the empaths of the world. You may be surprised once you realize just how thin the veil can be."

Jade shivered. "Yikes. Honestly, the idea gives me a bit of the creeps."

Madame Garnier chuckled. "Quite understandable. But I believe you may come to enjoy both communicating with the deceased and discovering ways to help them. Now, you mentioned a photograph and invitations?"

"Oh, yes. I'd love your thoughts. Please make yourself comfortable. Let me finish clearing the table and I'll fetch them."

Aidan put his arm out for Madame Garnier, while towering over the petite woman. "Why, aren't you the perfect gentleman, Aidan MacFie?"

He grinned while leading her to the sofa across from the fireplace. Jade joined them shortly afterward. She pointed to the portrait above the mantel, shaking her head.

"Well, this is the infamous painting I told you about. The Scottish laird disappeared a few days ago. A lady in grey replaced the mysterious figure. Incredibly, the woman appeared to move just over an hour ago. She's turned her back and, stepped closer to the shore. And now she's holding a satchel and kerosene lamp. Aidan and I watched the changes shortly before you arrived."

Madame Garnier's gnarled fingers reached toward her throat when she gazed up at the portrait.

"Aww, I see what you're talking about. Simply fascinating. And monarchs, too. Interesting."

Jade scrolled through her phone. "Took some photos of the painting before its recent…metamorphosis," she said, pointing to her iPhone screen.

The elderly woman narrowed her eyes as she studied the images.

"An interesting choice of words, considering the monarchs in the distance. And what an odd coincidence that butterflies helped track down Aidan during his abduction. I recall you discovered your poor husband in an abandoned house near the Monarch Sanctuary."

Jade shuddered, recalling the memory.

"Yes, I dreamed about monarch butterflies the night before. In fact, I jotted down the dream the next morning. It prompted me to drive around Pacific Grove, hoping to find some clue concerning Aidan's disappearance. I left the cottage near dawn, spending most of the day searching. After several hours without leads, I was about to head home when I noticed a swarm of butterflies heading toward the Monarch Sanctuary. Thankfully, I took your advice about listening to my hunches. When I noticed Morrigan perching on the roof of an abandoned house nearby, I climbed the fence to take a closer look. I glanced through a dirty window in the back of the home and was stunned to see Aidan inside. I tried to call for help, but my phone died. And that's when those terrible men grabbed me and took me prisoner. My timing was terrible. Aidan was in the process of escaping, but after his kidnappers grabbed me, I ruined his chance."

Aidan placed his arm around his wife's slender waist, kissing her temple."

"It all worked out in the end. And I discovered Jade's impressive detective skills. But I agree," he said, studying the portrait. "The continuous changes to the canvas are shocking."

Jade nodded. "Mary warned us on the plane ride home from Tobermory that the portrait changed back to its previous incarnation. Honestly, we were hoping to be finished with all these strange events once the Hunters were arrested."

"Something or someone desires your attention, mademoiselle. Perhaps even your assistance," Madame Garnier said, reaching down to give Dougal a pat on the head. "Perhaps it will ease your mind to think of the portrait as a gift. The fact that the painting helped lead you to Aidan suggests it is most likely a benevolent spirit influencing the alterations."

Jade let out her breath, eyeing the portrait. "I sure hope so. I'd feel much better if I understood who the woman in the painting could be," she said, shaking her head. "Oh, I'd like to show you one more thing, Madame Garnier. I'll be right back."

Aidan watched his wife leave for the bedroom. A moment later, she returned with a box of heirlooms.

"Love your opinion concerning some unusual antiques I recently acquired. Forgot to mention them the day you stopped by the shop." She placed the mysterious photograph of the Edwardian woman and her companions on top of the living room table. "As you can see, it's quite unique. Also discovered a newspaper article which may be related," she said, placing a tarnished paper next to the framed photograph. And thirdly, this collection of Christmas Eve invitations was included with the shipment," Jade added, placing the cards next to the newspaper article. "Oddly, I don't remember ordering the items. They were shipped from a local Carmel estate sale. Things have been a bit odd at the cottage since I brought them home. Before I go into detail, I wonder if you might get a sense of anything unusual?"

"Of course," Madame Garnier said, her dark eyes full of curiosity.

When Jade handed the framed photograph to her friend, her demeanor immediately changed. Within moments, the color drained from Madame Garnier's face.

"Are you alright?" Jade asked.

Seeming to stare through her, Madame Garnier took a hesitant step backward.

"I think I need to sit down."

Before the psychic lost her balance, Aidan rushed to her side, gently helping her to the couch. Once she took her seat, the couple exchanged troubled looks.

"There is tragedy attached to this young woman in the photograph. Oh, God. Such loss…."

As Madame Garnier leaned back, her eyes rolled into their sockets and her lips pinched together. Dougal whimpered and nuzzled her cold hand. The psychic sat motionless for a nearly a full minute before speaking. When she finally opened her mouth, her voice took on a youthful cadence.

"Please let me out of this room! You can't leave me like this. Must have water. I'll perish if you don't come back!" She placed trembling hands to her temples and shuddered. In a voice just barely over a whisper, she continued her lament. "If only I could find my way to the sea, back to the cottage. Oh, how I yearn to see my beloved's face again! Please, God, someone help me!"

Thunder rumbled overhead and the living room lights flickered and shut off. The flames in the hearth rose in jagged peaks as a heavy wind pummeled the sides of the cottage. When Madame Garnier opened her eyes, she focused on the fire. Slowly, she regained her composure and begin to speak in her familiar voice once again.

"Beware of the soulless one. His eyes burn like yellow opals in the night."

"What do you mean, Madame Garnier?" Jade asked, sitting beside her friend. She took her hand, which was icy to the touch. In alarm, the couple watched the old woman's dark eyes roll back into their sockets. Dougal curled onto Madame Garnier's lap and licked her hand.

When Madame Garnier regained her composure, she sat up, fluttering her eyes wide open.

Jade gasped and instinctively pulled away. Aidan took his wife's hand as they watched the psychic's ebony eyes turn hazel.

When she spoke, it was in the stranger's voice, strained and weak.

"Where are you, my love? Johnathon? Can't see you in the dark. Please come back to me, darling. Who's there? Oh, God! Leave me alone. Don't touch me, demon!"

The elderly woman sunk against the couch cushion, her mouth agape.

Aidan took a seat next to her and gently reached for her wrist. He took her pulse, finding it racing beneath crepe skin.

"Madame Garnier! Can you hear me?" he asked.

Her eyes slowly opened, appearing ebony once again.

"Oh, my God, Madame Garnier. Are you alright? Jade asked, taking her other hand in hers."

The old woman feigned a smile and nodded.

"Yes, my dears. I'll be fine. Not sure about the poor soul on the other side. Afraid contact ended before I could find my answers. One thing is certain, however."

"What's certain?" Jade asked.

"Someone urgently needs our help."

⚜

AIDAN'S BROW FURROWED. "I THINK YOU SHOULD GO TO THE HOSPITAL, Madame Garnier. You're pale as a ghost," he said, pressing his fingers to her wrist. "Your pulse is racing; I think it would be best to get you seen by a doctor. Let me drive you to the hospital."

To his astonishment, the psychic laughed and patted his hand.

"No worries, young man. Assure you I'm perfectly fine. This is just part of the process of crossing the veil. Just need a sip of wine," she said, sitting up taller.

"Of course," Jade said, handing her a crystal of Cabernet from the living room table.

"Thank you, dear." She drained the glass and leaned back against the sofa.

"Imagine my appearance may have alarmed you. Spirit had much to say tonight. Afraid the poor soul is urgently searching for someone. Just terrible how her life ended tragically. And, of course, now there's the issue of the dark one." She tsked, before requesting another glass of wine.

Jade put her hand to her throat, gazing up at Aidan's concerned face. She fetched the bottle of Cabernet and refilled her friend's glass.

Once Madame Garnier finished her wine, Jade continued her line of questioning.

"Afraid I don't understand. Who is the dark one? Is there something evil attached to the photograph? If so, we should get rid of it. I don't want something like that in my house!" Jade said, moving toward the fireplace. "This is too much. A ghost is strange enough, but now you're suggesting something evil crossed over. Demonic energy? An unholy spirit?" Jade crossed herself and shuddered.

"Lass, I think you might have watched too many horror movies," Aidan said with a chuckle, trying to put his wife at ease.

Madame Garnier stood from the couch and joined Jade beneath the portrait. She took her hand and turned toward Aidan.

"Young man, I understand you want to make your wife feel better. It's only natural. Unfortunately, Jade's instincts are correct. We're not dealing with a simple haunting. It's evident there's more than just a harmless spirit attached to these objects. Probably should have warned you before I went under. Afraid I don't always have control of the entities surfacing during my sessions. There's always risks when crossing the veil," Madame Garnier said, turning toward Jade. "Bringing the objects to your home may have been a mistake. The fact you possess psychic abilities, although newly recognized, has tossed gasoline onto the fire. I sense a dark entity following the wandering female spirit, something evil. Since she's already reached out for help, it was just a matter of time before the dark half showed its presence. My visit just prompted it along. As well as the storm tonight," Madame Garnier said.

"What does the weather have to do with tonight's activity?" Jade asked.

"Thunder and lightning cause electrical disturbances between the veils. Spirits occasionally use storms to manifest, creating conduits between dimensions."

"Oh, boy. And we're due for some rough weather the next couple of weeks, according to the news," Aidan said, biting down on his lower lip. "I don't like this at all. Especially the fact that Jade's home alone when I'm at the station. How can I protect her from something I can't see?"

His wife took his hand and smiled. "Aidan, I don't want you to worry about me when you're at work. You have a dangerous job and don't need distractions. But I'd be lying if I said I wasn't disturbed by the possibility of an evil spirit in our house. It's beyond unnerving."

Aidan moved his wife against his brawny chest. "I'll never let anything harm you, love. Ye have my word. We'll figure this out." He turned to Madame Garnier. "I'm so sorry to have brought you into all of this. We just wanted to enjoy a lovely supper with you. Never imagined placing you in harm's way."

"That's quite alright, young man. It's not the first time I've looked into the eyes of evil, and I suspect it won't be the last before I depart this mortal coil. Now, I'll be just fine. Planning to pray the Rosary tonight. God is more powerful than any evil spirit. Have faith, children. I'm relieved I visited this evening. The presence in your home is much more serious than I originally believed. There are at least two souls connected to the portrait. Will need more time to meditate on it. Too weak to do any good tonight, but I will come back when you're ready. Be prepared for battle, young ones. You will be facing a choice soon. Energies tied from years ago have attached to both the portrait and photograph. Jade, your energy attracted a lost soul who's passed over a century ago. She's reaching out, asking for help. And something more sinister as well. It will be your decision how to proceed."

"If there's an evil presence, should I rid myself of the items?" Jade asked, wringing her hands.

"I'm afraid it would do no good at this stage. If you try to remove the antiques, it will only cause more disturbances between the veils. Don't worry, child. We will figure this out together. For now, say your prayers and be on guard until we attain more facts. It's important we find the origin of both the painting and photograph. Once we have this information, we can try contacting the spirits once more."

Jade glanced at Aidan's concerned face, then back to Madame Garnier's ashen one.

"Madame Garnier, Jade and I would feel much better if you were checked out at a hospital. You've been through an ordeal tonight," Aidan said.

The elderly woman placed her hand on his arm and smiled.

"Such a kind young man. Thank you, but I simply need to go home and rest with my precious cats. They are healers, you know?"

"Well, at least let us drive you home," Jade said.

"That will be fine," Madame Garnier agreed.

THE GREY LADY OF MONARCH COVE

Aidan nodded. "I really will feel better if you'd see a doctor."

"No. I'll be perfectly fine. Perhaps you can drive my car? I do feel a bit tired after the visitation this evening."

"Of course, Madame Garnier," Aidan said.

"Let me follow in the truck so my husband can drive back with me after he drops you off," Jade said, walking to the closet to retrieve Madame Garnier's coat, umbrella, and purse.

"Thank you, dear," their guest said, walking toward the door.

Aidan and Jade grabbed their coats and keys. Before they opened the front door, Morrigan flew to the couch, landing next to Dougal. The white raven snuggled up to the terrier and he gave her a lick.

"Do you think the pets will be safe by themselves?" Aidan asked.

"They look so comfortable together. It would be a shame to bother them. The presence is gone for now," Madame Garnier said.

"We'll be back in a little while, babies," Jade said, waving toward the animals. Dougal's tail wiggled, but he stayed cuddled against Morrigan.

The group braced themselves as they walked down the slippery cobblestone driveway. Heavy wind pulled at Aidan's umbrella as he ushered the women to their vehicles. After Jade started the truck, she watched the black Cadillac moving down the dark road, slivers of moonlight reflecting off its back windows. Tailing close behind, she flicked on the windshield wipers and heater. As Jade made her way down the familiar path, her mind raced while lightning streaked across the weeping sky.

৩⭑৩

HOSTING THEIR FIRST DINNER TOGETHER SEEMED LIKE A LOVELY distraction from the strange events taking place at the cottage. She'd hoped to discover clues relating to the portrait and vintage photograph from the shop. Unfortunately, their evening turned into a series of bizarre spectacles. Jade shuddered at the possibility of spirits taking refuge in her home. And she was not prepared for the psychic's channeling session. What exactly transpired tonight? It was one thing to read about supernatural phenomenon in books. Although she was a long-time horror fan, experiencing paranormal activity first-hand was beyond unsettling. Her stomach clenched when she remembered the way Madame Garnier's ebony eyes turned a startling hazel. And hearing the young, frightened voice escaping the psychic's lips turned her blood cold. Goosebumps rose on her skin despite the heater being turned up to full volume. What exactly had she witnessed? The voice of the deceased? Could this unknown spirit be connected to the phantom portrait or vintage photograph? Possibly both? It was beyond comprehension. And if so, what did the entity want? At least Aidan was a witness to the strange phenomenon. She didn't have to tackle the situation by herself. The couple had plenty to talk about when they returned home.

Hopefully, Madame Garnier would be fine after her experience. She'd feel better if her friend agreed to get checked out at the hospital. Yet, try as they might, the psychic was determined to go home to her cats. Jade blinked in response to a driver's approaching high beams, trying to make out the hazy road stretching before her. The remaining drive was unnerving, and it was a relief when she finally reached her destination. After parking, Jade watched the windshield wipers slice through torrents of rain, while Aidan escorted Madame Garnier with his umbrella. He waited on the porch while she fumbled for her keys inside her Victorian purse. When Madame Garnier opened the door, she was greeted by soft lamplight and an array of sleeky black cats. Jade smiled, remembering her feline companions during their first Tarot session. At the time, she believed the psychic to be an eccentric old lady. Little did she know how close they would become.

She shook her head and sighed. At least Madame Garnier would have her furry entourage to keep her company during the stormy night, she thought. Jade released her breath, hoping her friend would be safe after the paranormal encounter. A few moments later, Aidan opened the passenger side door of the truck. He took his wife in his arms, kissing her firmly on the mouth. With a soft smile, she smoothed back the damp locks from her husband's handsome face. After turning on the ignition, she pulled away from the curb. Noticing the rain gutters overflowing, she reduced her speed and focused intently on the flooding road.

Aidan shook his head. "Offered one last time to drive her to the hospital, but Madame Garnier refused. Aye, she's a stubborn one. Reminds me of a beautiful lass I know," he said, caressing Jade's cheek with the back of his left hand.

Jade nodded. "I'll check on her tomorrow morning. Wish she'd get checked out tonight but sounds like her mind's already made up."

"Well, I did make her promise to give us a call if she's not feeling well.

Pretty much shooed me away with a mischievous gleam in her eyes. Said she's going to make a hot toddy and curl up with a good book."

"What a remarkable woman. Hope I'm as feisty when I'm her age," Jade said, watching the windshield wipers slice through the curtain of rain.

"Something tells me you will be," Aidan said, studying his wife's profile. "Are you sure you're comfortable driving in this storm? Be more than happy to take the wheel."

Jade glanced at her husband with amusement. "I think I'm fine, but thank you," she said, turning her attention back to the road.

As they moved through downtown Pacific Grove, the newlyweds discussed their strange encounter with Madame Garnier. There was no doubt she'd made contact, even channeled the mysterious grey lady. If this was her first contact, what could they expect next? The question filled Jade with uneasiness. After she'd parked in front of the cottage, the couple hurried to the front porch. Hail peppered down, and it was a relief when they shut the door behind them. Once inside, they were greeted by a familiar blur of ebony fur. Dougal ran circles around the couple while Morrigan cawed from the couch ruffling her pearly feathers in the dimly lit room.

"Think I'm going to change into some flannel pajamas and get ready for bed. Tonight's worn me out," Jade said with a sigh.

"Good idea, love. I'll put some wood on the fire and join you in a minute."

Before Jade tended to her bedtime routine, she paused by the hallway. "Do you think Madame Garnier's going to be alright? I'm really worried about her," she said, chewing her bottom lip.

Aidan considered the question a moment before answering. "Aye, she's a stubborn Cailleach, but I believe she'll be fine," he said.

Jade's eyebrows rose. "Cailleach?"

"It's Scottish for old woman, darlin'".

"Aww, alright then," she answered with a smile.

After Jade changed into a pair of flannel pajamas and slippers, she headed to the kitchen to make a pot of cocoa. Before long, the comforting aroma of hot chocolate wafted through the cottage. Placing two ceramic mugs onto a silver platter, she headed to the living room table.

Once seated, Aidan moved his arm around his wife's shoulder, and they quietly sipped their beverages. While thunder boomed overhead, Jade gazed into her husband's loving eyes. Lost in their ocean blue depths, she felt his fingers weaving through her golden tresses. Firelight reflected the sheen of steel-grey eyes and his lips found hers. As her heart thrummed against his defined chest; Aidan lifted his wife into his powerful arms and carried her to the bedroom. Lightning flashed behind lace-covered windows while they made love to the sound of falling rain.

Chapter Six

JADE WOKE AN HOUR BEFORE AIDAN. AS SUNLIGHT SLIPPED THROUGH THE kitchen windows, she prepared a savory pot of coffee and a light breakfast of bagels and homemade jam. With anticipation, she relished the opportunity to enjoy a romantic weekend with her husband. Before setting the table, she called Madame Garnier. Finding her friend in good spirits, her anxiety lifted, and she was able to focus on the day ahead. After breakfast, the couple drove to Carmel with Dougal in the passenger seat. If the weather cooperated, they'd enjoy a lovely day of sightseeing, dining, and shopping. One of Jade's favorite getaways, the seaside town was a mere six miles from her home. With sudden clarity, she realized how often she'd taken for granted the unique opportunity to live near such picturesque surroundings. Starting up a small business, moving into a new home, along with her recent adventures with Aidan distracted her from the fact.

Carmel-by-the-Sea was a dog friendly town, so they made sure to bring Dougal. As they weaved their way through the scenic roadway, the terrier hung his head out the back of the Tahoe, enjoying breathtaking views along the oak-lined trees of the wealthy neighborhood. With just three thousand permanent residents, the town was a world-renowned tourist hotspot, boasting incredible beaches, shops, five-star restaurants, art galleries, golf courses, whimsical architecture, and luxurious neighborhoods. Not only was Carmel-by-the-Sea a wonderful weekend getaway, but Jade also enjoyed their frequent estate sales. When she couldn't find the time to visit, she hired a company called *Treasures in the Attic*. The convenience of shopping on their colorful website saved her both time and money. While she vacationed in Scotland, the company had delivered several boxes from an order she'd made the previous summer. Interestingly, a few "extras" were included, most notably the photograph of the lady in grey.

Combing through the quiet streets of Carmel-by-the-Sea, they passed storybook homes nestled beneath shady cypress trees. They turned on Ocean Avenue, admiring a long stretch of cafés, shops, and art galleries. Continuing along Scenic Road, their tour included a cross-section of sprawling mansions overlooking the azure sea, separated by a narrow one-way road.

"These properties are gorgeous. How nice to have access to private beaches. The homeowners are just yards away from the white sandy shore," Jade said.

"It's lovely," Aidan agreed. "If I remember correctly, there are several homes right on the water. Although, I believe the terrain is not as hospitable as the beach by our cottage."

As the road took a steep turn, the couple noticed a smoky grey gothic mansion sheltered within a private cove. Rocky terrain replaced the flat beachfront properties. Although the estate was mere yards from the seashore, it lacked the accessible white sands of the previous properties.

As Jade studied the cresting waves crashing along the rugged shore, an ominous feeling darkened her mood.

"It's impossible," Jade whispered, placing her hand on Aidan's arm.

He glanced over in alarm. "What's wrong, love?"

She hesitated a moment before answering. "Do you mind parking next to the home with the overgrown lawn?" she asked, pointing toward a massive estate encircled by a wrought iron gate. Twisted cypress trees lined the perimeter of the property.

"Of course."

They found a parking space out front, and the couple stepped out into the cold, damp morning. Aidan waited patiently for his wife to gather her thoughts. Pulling her navy peacoat around her slender shoulders, she moved toward the weathered iron fence adorned with jet-black spikes rising toward the heavens.

"This is going to sound crazy, but you're probably used to that by now..." she trailed off.

After a moment of quiet contemplation, she released her breath. Jade realized the estate was the same one from her dreams. Without a doubt, the steeply pitched roof and lacy bargeboards matched her vision. Being familiar with the gothic architecture from numerous art history classes, she'd grown to love the style. The precipitous canopy of the mansion, windows adorned with pointed arches, lacy bargeboards, and the one-story porch cemented her assumption. Looking closer, she noted steep cross gables, bay and oriel windows, and vertical board and batten siding, suggesting a Carpenter Gothic estate.

Aidan studied his wife's face, sensing her trepidation. Trying to lighten the mood, he took her hand and chuckled.

"Your beautiful imagination is one of the things I love about you, lass. Ye keep me guessing."

She gazed into his loving eyes. His steadfast devotion and non-judgmental nature allowed her to freely express herself. Jade stepped closer, blinking in the fog.

"Afraid I've been having vivid dreams again."

"Hmm, I can't say I'm surprised. Been tossing and turning in your sleep. Figured you might be having some nightmares. I was afraid to wake you. Didn't know if it would frighten you if I did."

She nodded. "Yes, I've had some restless nights. Dreamed of this exact house. It's crazy, but my dream appeared to take place in a different era." She chewed her bottom lip, wringing her gloved hands together. "I remember a feeling of antiquity. It appeared much grander, the estate and grounds. The home was well-kept, not a blade of grass out of place."

Squinting in the hazy mist, she stepped closer to the wrought iron gate, peering through the open spaces. "And to make it even stranger..."

"What's that, darlin'?" Aidan asked, pushing back a lock of golden curls from her pale forehead.

"Can't be sure without looking through some old receipts, but I believe this might be the property where my last batch of antiques originated. I'm certain they were from a Carmel estate sale. If I remember correctly, the original order was divided into two shipments."

"Oh?"

"Yes. Do you remember when you first arrived at the shop when my alarm went off?"

"Of course, lass. How could I ever forget?"

She smiled up into his sparkling eyes.

"Me too. Well, the first shipment arrived shortly before we met. Then, the second order arrived when we were in Scotland."

"Interesting," Aidan said.

"I'm not completely sure, but I believe this might be the house listed from *Treasures in the Attic*. The company I've been using to purchase estate sale items."

"Oh, the same order with the mysterious photograph?"

"Afraid so. You see, the items were auctioned on their website months ago; the pieces originated from a gothic-style mansion located in Carmel," Jade said, scrolling through her phone. "Maybe I can find the address from my order receipt. I believe there's a copy in my email."

"Well, it might be a little tricky looking up the address."

Jade stopped scrolling and her brows raised. "What do mean?"

"The funny thing about these lovely homes in Carmel is that there are no street addresses. One of the many oddities concerning the town. Apparently, the original settlers wanted to get to know their neighbors," Aidan said.

"Oh, that's right! I forgot. I remember reading an article about Carmel's eccentric history," Jade said.

"Yes, the town's founding fathers feared their village would become 'citified,' so they proposed a central post office instead of house-to-house delivery. There's no residential addresses, streetlights, sidewalks, or parking meters. Although, I understand the commercial area doesn't abide to these rules," Aidan said.

"Carmel-by-the-Sea has such a fascinating past. I'd love to learn more," Jade said.

"Aye, it does. There's a historical center in town if you want to do some research. So, does the estate sale mention a name, maybe, or cross street?" Aidan asked.

"Oh, good question," Jade said, combing through her purse. With iPhone in hand, she scrolled through her emails. After a few minutes, her eyes widened in disbelief.

"Yes, my order came from a property called *Monarch Cove*. It's located off Scenic Road. This must be the same estate I purchased my auction items. From what I understand, the owner was an elderly woman. She passed last summer, and the property's been on the market ever since. Appears there's some flyers in front of the home," she said, pointing toward a plastic container hanging near the gate. "Maybe it will give us more information." Jade walked over and reached for one of the colorful listings. "Wow, it's listed considerably low for the area. Can't believe it's still available. And so close to the sea," Jade said.

"Aye, it's definitely selling under market," Aidan said, brows furrowing. "Of course, it looks like it could use some work," he said, eyeing the dreary estate. "Seems like it's been left to the elements, but there's plenty of fixer-uppers that go for much more in the area."

The home was a massive building, protected by a lengthy wrought iron gate which prevented curious tourists wandering about the property. A band of sunlight penetrated the thick cloud cover; Jade's eyes rose to the pointed spheres rising toward the heavens. The muted sunlight quickly disappeared behind storm clouds. The charcoal grey paint of the mansion matched the oppressive skies above. The contrast to the storybook cottages along the road was startling. The estate appeared to have been plucked from a Brontë novel and deposited into the quiet neighborhood.

Despite the ominous presentation, Jade was intrigued to learn more about the property. She wouldn't be satisfied until she could look inside the mysterious home for herself. She placed her hand onto the gate's rusty door handle and quickly realized it was locked.

"Imagine you'll need to reach out to the agent if you want to peek inside," Aidan said.

"Hmm, what do you think the odds of getting a showing today?" Jade asked.

Aidan studied his wife's hopeful eyes, knowing he'd do anything to make her happy.

"You're getting one of your feelings, aren't ye, love?"

"Afraid so, but I don't want to interrupt our date. Perhaps we should try another day..." Jade said, trying to rein in her excitement.

"Don't ye worry about spoiling our weekend," Aidan said, lifting her small hand to his lips. She flushed at his gentle touch. He chuckled, pleased he could invoke her passion so easily.

"Every minute spent with my blushing bride is an absolute pleasure," he said with a grin. "I don't mind at all. And I've learned never to ignore my wife's hunches."

As they turned to leave, Dougal whimpered and pulled toward the iron partition. His ebony hackles rose as he released a low growl. His head cocked sideways, pulling at his tether, edging closer to the yard.

"What's wrong, buddy? Is there a cat nearby?" Jade asked with a smile. But her lighthearted tone disappeared when she lifted her gaze toward the mansion.

Jade put her hand to her throat. "Oh, my God," she whispered.

"What's wrong?" Aidan asked.

"Don't you see it?" she asked, pointing to the upper window on the second floor.

Her husband stared in confusion. "Sorry, love. What am I looking for exactly?"

Jade squinted in the muted daylight, noting the silhouette of a woman in the window. The wispy outline suggested an Edwardian gown, tailored neatly across a tiny waist and hour-glass figure. Brunette curls rested beneath a large grey bonnet, tied in a dainty silk bow beneath her delicate chin. She watched in awe as a slender hand grazed across the curtain. With a flutter of ivory lace, the image dissolved beneath the muted sky.

Jade turned toward her husband and shook her head. "There was a lady at the window, but she's gone now. Appeared to have vanished."

Aidan's mouth drew down at the corners. "Didn't notice, darlin', but I believe you. Let's get some brunch and we'll see if we can get a showing this afternoon. Maybe we'll find some answers inside."

"Good idea. It's funny, but I feel drawn to this house somehow."

"Then we will take a closer look. But let's do it on a full stomach," he said, flashing his inviting smile. "There's a nice café I know with wonderful views. Fairly sure they'll have vegan options."

Jade glanced up and smiled.

"That does sound nice."

With the wind to their backs, Aidan escorted Jade back to the SUV before heading over to a nearby café.

They waited in line for several minutes before being seated outside by the waiter. The twenty-something server sported an impressive man-bun and matching auburn beard. Smiling, he gestured for the couple to follow.

Aidan took Jade's hand as they were led down a stairway toward a table facing the sea. Seagulls cried, occasionally diving toward the churning waves. A raft of sea otters floated nearby. One pair held hands as they dozed together beneath the hazy sky. A sliver of sunlight sliced through the cloud cover, warming their upturned bellies. Jade grinned, realizing how lucky they were living among such incredible wildlife. She'd never tire from all the splendors Monterey County offered. Sitting back in her steel chair, she sighed and reached for Aidan's large hand. His aquamarine eyes appeared unearthly against the charcoal skies.

"Does this suit you? It's been a while since I stopped in, but they had a fantastic chef last time I visited," Aidan said, handing his wife a menu.

"Oh, yes. It's lovely. And I'm starving. A mocha would be perfect with this chilly weather." She noticed an outdoor fireplace nearby. Feeling cozy, Jade reclined in her chair and released her pent-up breath. They studied the menu a few moments, then their server returned to take their order. His shock of auburn hair reminded Jade of many of the inhabitants of Scotland. She'd never witnessed so many redheads in her life.

After a bit of a wait, the server returned with their drinks and two orders of avocado toast, along with a potato scramble with mixed vegetables. Despite the lovely atmosphere, Jade's mind kept wandering back to the mysterious gothic mansion. She took a bite of avocado and washed it down with a sip of creamy mocha. While they finished up their meal, Aidan scrolled through his iPhone searching for local real-estate agents. After determining a match, he excused himself from the table to make a call. Several minutes passed while Jade waited in nervous anticipation. She couldn't lock down the source of her anxiety but hoped seeing the inside of the gothic estate would ease her mind somehow.

Aidan returned to the table with a wide grin. "Good news, love. I've arranged a meeting with an agent. Booked her at one this afternoon if it suits ye." He folded muscular arms on the table while giving his wife the news.

"That's perfect! Figured we might have to wait a bit. What a lovely surprise," Jade said, taking a sip of her coffee.

"Well, it's Saturday, and this area is probably full of eager buyers. Maybe the agent was already planning a showing today," Aidan said.

"Maybe," Jade said, dotting her mouth with her napkin. The couple made small talk while they waited for their appointment. Dougal pulled at his leash, eager to be off. He'd enjoyed several treats from his master's pocket while they dined. Jade loved her husband's thoughtfulness, especially when it came to their pets.

"Alright, buddy," Aidan said, standing from his chair. Jade took her husband's arm and they headed back to their vehicle. An icy breeze chilled her skin and tears prickled her steel-grey eyes as they made their way down the damp sidewalk. While she breathed in the balmy aroma of the sea, Jade's mind swirled with a list of questions she intended to pepper the real-estate agent.

When they headed toward the scenic seaside once again, the weather took a turn for the worse. Although traffic was thick that day, they had no trouble finding a parking lot in front of the mansion. With the number of tourists in Carmel, parking spots were coveted. Jade found it odd that the road was lined with cars, apart from Monarch Cove. Jade snapped a tether to Dougal's harness and his short legs bounded out onto the empty pathway. Once again, she gazed up at the mysterious home. A collection of onyx clouds gathered above the gothic estate while several ebony crows balanced on the pointed garrets, their shiny wings fluttering in the breeze. Jade believed the scene looked something right out of a horror movie, but kept the thought to herself. She glanced at the window where she'd noticed the apparition earlier in the day, but the opaque glass appeared empty.

Aidan placed his hand against the small of her back and led her toward the wrought iron gate. Moments later, massive mahogany doors opened toward the front of the mansion. A set of marble stairs led down toward an overgrown pathway, cutting across a collection of crabgrass and wild jasmine. Trails of creeping ivy covered the beams of the white-washed porch and sides of the home. A petite elderly woman waved from the top of the stairs. Jade smiled, noticing her brightly colored pantsuit. The canary yellow fabric matched her horned-rimmed glasses. A ray of sunlight reflected the thick lenses. Despite her advanced age, the realtor moved gracefully across the cobblestone pathway dividing the overgrown lawn.

With a bit of an effort, she clicked a skeleton key into the gated lock. With a groan to its hinges, the partition opened, and she gestured for the couple to enter. Once they'd stepped through to the other side, she locked the barrier behind them.

"There we go," she said, turning to Aidan with a smile. "Safety first. We've recently had some trespassers on the estate. Been quite a lot of interest since the property went on the market." Her gravelly voice hinted she was an avid smoker. She turned to study her guests with interest. "Such a lovely young couple. I'm Abby Dunsmuir."

"Nice to meet you, Mrs. Dunsmuir. I'm Jade MacFie and this is my husband Aidan," she said, trying not to stare at the agent's unusually pale-blue eyes. The thick bottlecap lenses made them appear grotesquely large in comparison to her narrow face.

"Welcome to Monarch Cove!"

"Monarch Cove?" Jade asked with curiosity.

"Why, yes. The original owner named the estate in the early 1900's. It was common to appoint titles for mansions back in the day. And this particular property lives up to its namesake. There's a lovely cove behind the house with spectacular views and beachfront access."

"Sounds gorgeous," Jade said.

The elderly woman nodded, glancing down at Dougal. He sniffed the front porch with interest.

"What a sweet dog. Scottish Terrier?"

"Aye," Aidan said with a smile. "His name's Dougal. I'm afraid we were not planning on visiting homes today. Would it be possible to bring him inside while we look at the place? Or the backyard would be fine of course. We don't like leaving him behind in the car. The pup gets a wee bit agitated by himself."

"Of course. Carmel-by-the-Sea has always been a dog loving community. It's been like that since I was a little girl. Oh, I had the most beautiful little dachshund years ago. Her name was Daisy. Followed me everywhere, so it was just wonderful taking her to the shops and galleries downtown. Before I realized it, she'd become a regular at all my favorite haunts. My darling Daisy was the love of my life. Broke my heart when she passed; I never even considered getting another dog," she said, smiling down at Dougal. "Why don't you bring him inside? It's awfully chilly today." The realtor glanced up and sighed. "Oh, my. Feels like it's going to rain any minute now," she said, glancing at the ominous clouds pressing down over the charcoal-grey skyline. "Don't want to get the poor boy soaked," Mrs. Dunsmuir said, gesturing them inside.

Aidan glanced up and nodded. "Aye, it does look like we're getting ready for a downpour. Thank you."

Just as they were about to cross the threshold, Dougal whimpered, pulling tightly against his tether before plopping down on his haunches.

Aidan frowned. "What's the matter, boy?"

After a moment of hesitation, the Scottish Terrier gingerly stepped inside the mansion. With Dougal in the lead, the couple followed the elderly woman across the black and white marble entryway into a large parlor adorned with nineteenth century furniture. The agent retrieved a set of glossy pamphlets set on top of the Edwardian cherry wood table.

"I'm thrilled to give you a showing. Before we get started, let me give you each a pamphlet containing a more detailed look at the property. The flyers outside only hint at the remarkable qualities of the estate," she said, suppressing a raspy cough with the back of her hand.

"Pardon me," she said, and handed the couple the paperwork.

Before continuing the tour, she reached into a clutch purse, canary yellow like the rest of her outfit, and retrieved a tin of cough drops. She popped a lozenge between her chapped lips and continued.

"I'm not contagious," she said, pushing the cough drop toward the back of her mouth with her tongue. Jade noticed a hint of eucalyptus wafting off the realtor, and the stronger scent of stale cigarettes lingering underneath.

"I've been smoking for nearly fifty years. God, I've tried to quit a hundred times!" she said, crossing her arms over her modest bosom. "Darn things. I guess I should be lucky I still have a voice after all these years," she said with a wide grin.

Jade involuntarily stepped backwards at the sight of the agent's yellowed teeth. Her eyes wandered over her gaunt face, and unusually pale eyes. She wondered if Aidan noticed her curious appearance. The frail woman barely seemed to have the strength to stand upright, let alone the fortitude to sell houses. Jade mused, she couldn't be more than ninety pounds soaking wet. If she was anything like her grandmother, it might be simple stubbornness keeping her going. It suddenly occurred to her that the agent's tarnished smile matched her outfit, and she mentally chastised herself for noticing.

It was difficult to ignore the realtor's exuberant mannerisms, which mirrored her departed family member. Grams had been an avid smoker herself from the age of sixteen. As luck had it, she'd passed from completely unrelated causes. Or so the doctor implied. Ironically, her mother who never touched, what she called 'coffin nails', succumbed to cancer at the considerably young age of forty-five.

Jade did not like where her thoughts were going. If she wasn't careful, she'd find herself back on the slippery slope of melancholia. She had barely made herself leave her bed the week after her mother's funeral. Only by the support of her friends had she found herself on the other side of grief. Immersing herself into a risky business venture and relocating to a new city had helped keep her distracted.

But here she was again, experiencing those old barbs of despair. There were too many coincidences she just couldn't ignore; something about the agent reminded her of her beloved grandmother. Like the fact she never went anywhere without her tin of cough drops. The combination of the tarnished scent of tobacco smoke and tangy eucalyptus brought back a rush of memories. Chewing at her bottom lip, Jade tried to rein in her emotions. Wasn't it funny how the smallest things could remind her of her loss, like a sharp punch to the gut? It was not even a year since she'd said goodbye to her mother. Sadly, she was just getting used to the fact her grandmother passed when her mom was diagnosed with an aggressive form of cancer. It seemed like only yesterday. Without realizing, her manicured fingernails pinched into her palms, forming white crescents. What she wouldn't give to hear their voices again, to call them up on her phone one last time. Grief, she'd discovered, was the gift that kept on giving. A slew of memories flashed by. Trying to ignore the unexpected emotions, she focused instead on the realtor's business card.

"Abby Dunsmuir, I see you're a local historian as well?" Jade asked, trying to keep her voice steady. Her husband glanced at his wife in concern, noticing the slight tremor in her voice. Aidan placed his hand on the small of her back and she released her pent-up breath.

"Yes, I'm quite the history buff, Mrs. MacFie. I'm semi-retired, but still find the time to tour some of the 'colorful' estates in the area," she said, making air quotes.

"That's fantastic. I'm quite a fan of antiquity myself. In fact, I recently finished my master's degree in art history, so I'd love to hear more about the historical side of the property."

Jade considered the elderly woman, trying to decide if she should let her know her true motive in touring the home. She glanced at her husband before speaking.

"And, truthfully, I should tell you we had another interest in the estate other than purchasing."

"Oh?" Abby's brows raised.

"You see, I own an antique shop in Pacific Grove. This may come as a surprise, but I purchased several pieces from this property last summer. My husband and I came across Monarch Cove purely by accident this morning. Once I realized it was the same mansion from the estate sale, I couldn't help but want to learn more," Jade said.

"Well, that makes perfect sense. Can't blame you for wanting to have a look inside. Oh, this house holds many secrets and scandals! If you love history, it's right up your alley, young lady. It's a curious home. Ah, if only the walls could talk…" she whispered, cracked lips drawing together.

"Really? Gothic architecture is one of my favorite styles. I'd love to learn more about the history," she said, glancing around the parlor. Jade noted the well-preserved antiquity, sensing she was slipping back in time.

"Well, it may interest you that this property is so much more than just your average Gothic-style manor," the elderly woman said, absently pushing her bifocals to the bridge of her narrow nose. When she took a step closer, the sharp odor of stale cigarettes prickled Jade's eyes, but she pretended not to notice. "And there's no need to apologize if you're not interested in purchasing. Like I said before, I'm a local historian."

The agent's smile faltered as she moved toward the fireplace. A set of crystal vases filled with sunflowers adorned each end of the mahogany mantel. Abby reached her age-spot covered hand toward the flowers closest to her, caressing a bright yellow petal. Tear-shaped droplets rolled down her gnarled fingers as she grazed the edges. "Of course, it's been some time since I've been able to properly research," she said, her voice taking on a wistful quality. "Sometimes I just don't know where the time goes…"

The realtor turned her back to the couple, lost in thought. Nearly a full minute passed before she spoke again. Jade glanced at Aidan, and they locked eyes as the uncomfortable silence stretched on.

Seeming to recover, Abby offered a wan smile. "Well, now, let's explore, shall we?"

"Thank you, Mrs. Dunsmuir. It's kind of you," Jade said.

"Before I get started, you mentioned you enjoy antiques and art history? Abby said, her pale blue eyes widening. "I'd love to hear more about your hobby."

"Of course. Well, I opened a shop in Pacific Grove last summer. Interestingly, one of my first orders originated from this property. The antiques arrived in two shipments. The second one arrived last week."

"That's lovely. Yes, I remember there were two separate estate sales. One took place last summer. If I remember correctly, it wasn't long after the owner passed away. Many of her beloved items went up for auction. Not all, however. I'll get to that in a moment if you're curious."

"Interesting," Jade said, sensing a story behind the mansion. "Love to hear more. The second shipment from Monarch Cove arrived when we were abroad. There were a couple unusual pieces I've been curious about."

"Abroad?"

"Yes, we just came back from Scotland," Aidan said.

"Oh, how exciting," Abby said, placing her palms together. "I noticed a bit of an accent, Mr. MacFie." After a moment of silence, she turned her attention to Jade.

"Well, now. Since you mentioned your interest in antiques, there's some real gems I think you'll positively adore. Each piece holds unique clues regarding the tale I'm about to share. Of course, with history sometimes comes tragedy. There's a shadow of superstition surrounding Monarch Cove. Oh, yes indeed. Quite the riveting narrative." Mrs. Dunsmuir locked eyes with Jade, gesturing her to follow.

"Really? I had no idea," Jade said, following close behind.

"Well, I should let you know this property has a dark past. Oh, if only walls could talk. If you listen carefully, the manor may whisper a sorrowful story."

Aidan raised his brow, looking around the room.

Abby Dunsmuir crossed the marble floor, stopping before a wall covered in framed vintage photographs. "Sadly, some valuable heirlooms were auctioned off during the estate sale last summer. Oh, such a shame to think of the pieces scattered to the wind." Abby threw her slender arms in the air and rolled her pale eyes.

"Thankfully, my favorite portrait remains! And what a story goes along with it. Ah, yes. It's a true gem." She grinned, revealing tobacco-stained dentures.

Aidan glanced at Jade and gave her a wink. She wondered if he found Abby Dunsmuir as entertaining as she did.

"Was the company involved in the auction called *Treasures in the Attic* by chance?" Jade asked.

"Yes, that sounds familiar. Once the auctioneers were hired, many price-less pieces were sold for pennies on the dollar. Oh, if only I'd could have stopped it," she said, her gravelly voice quivering. "But, alas, like Lady Macbeth so eloquently confessed, 'what's done is done.'"

Abby folded her arms over her narrow chest and closed her eyes.

Jade, sensing the woman's agitation, tried to change the subject.

"Mrs. Dunsmuir, you mentioned an interesting history attached to Monarch Cove? I'd love to hear more about it if you have the time. You see, I discovered an unusual photograph in a shipment last week."

"Is it of a lovely young lady sitting on the porch by chance?"

"Oh, yes! Have you seen it?"

"I've been looking for that photograph for months. It was quite special to me."

"Really? I'd be happy to bring it back if you'd like."

The elderly woman shook her head. "That's kind, young lady. I'm sure it has a charming new home with you. Although, I'd love to get my hands on a rather unique seascape which went missing last summer. Don't suppose one arrived at your shop by chance?" she asked, her penciled-in eyebrows arching into startling triangles.

Jade glanced at Aidan, and he shrugged his shoulders. She had a sinking feeling the agent might be referring to the portrait back at the cottage.

"Well, I didn't order any paintings from Monarch Cove. Most of the items are antique cups and teapots. However, I discovered a mysterious portrait in my shop's broom closet when I was unpacking my merchandise last October. I'm sure it wasn't included in the original shipment. How it ended up in the shop I have no idea. Been curious about it ever since," Jade said.

"Oh?" the agent said, stepping closer. "That's odd. Is the painting an ocean scene by chance? Surrounded by a gilded frame?"

Jade felt her stomach tighten. *How could she answer truthfully? After all, it was a seascape of sorts. The figures just kept changing. The lone man, who once stood by the sea, had vanished. In his place was a grey lady surrounded by a shroud of monarch butterflies.*

"Yes. The frame is quite ornate, and the painting depicts an exquisite seascape. The portrait features a Scottish laird in front of a castle by the sea."

Jade withheld telling her about the portrait's bizarre changes. How could she explain the original figure was replaced by an Edwardian lady? The agent would think she was joking.

Abby shook her head in disappointment. "Oh, no, that's not right. The painting I'm thinking of is an enchanting scene representing the Pacific Ocean. And there's no figures, just a modest cabin in the distance. From my understanding, it belonged to the original owner of Monarch Cove. You see, Deidre O'Shea was working on the painting shortly before she disappeared. It's unfinished. I imagine the canvas might fetch a hefty price considering its dark history. But how could I ever sell it? It would be like giving away an old friend!"

Jade feigned a smile, confused by the agent's meaning. What on earth is she talking about? she thought to herself.

"Deidre O'Shea?" Jade said, unfamiliar with the name.

"Why, yes. Surprised you haven't heard the legend of Monarch Cove," Abby said with a frown.

"No, I'm afraid I haven't. Moved to Pacific Grove just last summer. As I mentioned earlier, I ordered directly from *Treasures in the Attic*. Normally, I enjoy visiting local estate sales before acquiring, but just didn't have the time."

"Makes perfect sense. It's amazing how much can be done online these days." The agent pushed her bifocals to the bridge of her nose with a trembling hand. "Of course, I've never been computer savvy. Like to keep to the old ways."

After a moment of silence, Abby turned to the couple and smiled.

"Rumors have swirled around Monarch Cove for decades. In fact," she said, lowering her voice. "There's been sightings of a mysterious grey lady roaming about the property. Some say the mistress of the manor never left."

Jade released her breath, her mind immediately drawn to the painting above her own fireplace. If there was a mysterious grey woman, could she be pictured in both the portrait and the strange sighting in the upstairs window of the mansion? Although overwhelmed, she knew it was imperative to stay calm if she was going to get to the bottom of this mystery. Feeling Aidan's fingers interlacing hers filled her with a sense of relief. She wasn't alone. Together, they would figure things out.

"Well, it all sounds fascinating. If you have the time, we'd enjoy learning more," she said, nodding to her husband.

"Aye, we love a ghost story. If we're not keeping you, Mrs. Dunsmuir, we'd enjoy hearing your tale."

Abby returned his smile. "Why don't we start our tour by viewing the portrait of Lady O'Shea? After all, she's the heart of the home…"

With raised brows, Jade glanced over at her husband. Aidan placed his hand on the small of her back as they followed the realtor through a maze of interconnecting rooms. While their footsteps echoed across black and white marbled floors, the couple admired the richly adorned furniture and artwork. Booming thunder mingled with a mysterious scratching sound reverberating from the pitched ceiling. It wasn't until Jade noticed the rose-colored windows above the parlor, she understood the source of the noise. Gnarled willow branches moved in the roaring wind. Resembling twisted claws, their jagged edges scraped the glossy surface of the stained glass, sounding like nails on a chalkboard. She shivered. Once they reached the back of the spacious room, the couple gazed toward a high wall dividing two adjacent circular staircases. Between ruby-stained windows rested an ornately framed portrait of a dark-haired woman adorned in Edwardian attire. Hazel eyes appeared to follow their movements as they approached. For a moment, Jade noticed the faint aroma of jasmine, but it vanished soon after.

The agent turned toward Jade with a wan smile shadowing her narrow face.

"Please let me introduce you to the lady of the house, Mrs. Deidre O'Shea."

Jade's throat tightened as her eyes rose to the portrait.

It's impossible, she thought to herself, trying to keep a cool head. It's the same woman in the photograph. Her bright eyes and heart-shaped face are identical.

Moving closer, she studied the portrait with apprehension.

There was something curious about the young lady's expression. Her familiar upturned mouth hinted at a smile, but her bright eyes told another story. With the detailed sheen of her silver gown, one could imagine feeling its smooth satin between the pads of fingertips. A matching bonnet set atop brunette ringlets framed an angelic face. Standing with her back to the sea, doe-like eyes hinted at a secret life. Why does she seem so troubled? Jade thought. She was young and beautiful, obviously wealthy being the mistress of a grand estate. Why does she appear like a fragile bird trapped inside a gilded cage?

"It's incredible. Do you know anything about the work?" Jade asked.

Mrs. Dunsmuir's pale eyes shone with purpose. "There's quite a bit of superstition surrounding the portrait, Mrs. MacFie. I'm curious to hear your thoughts considering your art history background. Wouldn't you say it's haunting?"

Jade moved closer to the portrait, considering the fine details.

"Yes, it's gorgeous. If I were to take a guess, I'd say the painting was completed during the Edwardian period considering Deidre O'Shea's gown. Stylistically, it appears to belong to the Romantic era if I've not mistaken."

The agent nodded, impressed by Jade's observations.

"Excellent. Right on both accounts," Abby said with a wide grin, flashing tobacco-stained dentures.

Jade tried her best not to stare at the woman's discolored teeth. Instead, she turned her attention back to the portrait.

The agent pushed her bifocals to the bridge of her narrow nose, studying the couple with interest. After a moment of hesitation, she continued, "Full disclosure; I should let you know rumors have been floating around for decades concerning the young bride of Monarch Cove."

Jade glanced over at her husband, and he squeezed her hand.

"It's been a subject of curiosity, the source of many urban legends in town. Lady Deidre O'Shea disappeared on Christmas Eve, 1906, and the case was never solved."

"Disappeared?" Jade asked.

"Indeed. Quite the story if you're interested. Perhaps you'll join me in the kitchen? Just made a fresh pot of tea."

Aidan glanced down at his wife. "Sounds wonderful."

"Very good." The elderly woman gestured the couple to follow her back into a cheery breakfast nook where bay windows overlooked an expansive shore.

"Oh, this is quite lovely," Jade said, admiring the old-fashioned charm.

"Why don't you have a seat by the dining table beneath the window. There's a lovely view of Monarch Cove. And if you look carefully, you'll notice the same seascape background from the portrait of Lady O'Shea. It's where the young artist had her sit for him; and I imagine it's where they fell in love."

Jade held her breath, eager to hear more about the mysterious mistress of the manor. For the next two hours, they were told a haunting story of love, loss, and unsolved mysteries.

Chapter Seven

Aidan pulled out his wife's seat before taking his own. As thunder boomed, Dougal whimpered and climbed beneath his master's chair.

"What's wrong, Buddy?" Aidan said, reaching down to scratch behind the terrier's pointy ears. "You don't usually mind storms."

"Poor little guy," Jade said, watching the pup rest his fuzzy muzzle on his front paws. Once he seemed settled, she glanced around the room, admiring the antique feel. A lace-covered ivory tablecloth covered the oak dining table. A crystal vase overflowing with cheery sunflowers brightened the darkened room. Abby set a silver platter down, along with a floral-colored teapot and matching porcelain cups. Jade realized she'd purchased a similar set from the estate earlier in the year.

Rain pattered the bay windows as Abby Dunsmuir filled their cups with herbal tea. For a moment, the group sat in silence, listening to the haunting call of a cuckoo clock down the hall.

Once the elderly woman took her seat, the couple readied themselves for a spooky tale.

"Well, I guess I should start at the beginning. Just to give a bit of back-story, the town of Carmel was founded in 1902, and incorporated ten years later. It was officially named Carmel-by-the Sea in 1925.

"Our story begins in 1906. Interestingly, the same year of the infamous San Francisco Earthquake. Before I get ahead of myself, I should mention that the year prior, 1905, the Carmel Arts and Craft Club was founded. This is an important element which I'll circle back to.

"On a balmy February afternoon in 1906, a wealthy banker by the name Mr. Thomas O'Shea, married a working-class girl named Deidre Doyle. The teenager was orphaned at the tender age of seventeen. After her parents' deaths, the young lady apprenticed as a seamstress at her aunt's shop downtown. Her mother's sister, Hannah, was awarded temporary guardianship.

"From my understanding, Hannah officiated as a matchmaker of sorts between her niece and Mr. O'Shea. At the time, the banker was a well-sought-after bachelor. Leaving behind the generational legacy of a family immersed in the carpentry trade, the Irish immigrant sought his fortune in the States. Through a series of cunning business dealings, he established himself both property owner of several land holdings, along with acquiring the title of acting manager of Carmel Bank in the early 1900's. Deidre Doyle's aunt was said to have made a handsome profit by providing the matchmaking service between the two. In those days, the classes were divided, and it caused quite a bit of talk in town. But the young bride was charming, as well as beautiful, and the gossip eventually died down.

"Before the marriage was finalized, rumors swirled concerning the bride's reluctance. Despite her fiancé's prestige, the young woman had reservations. Thomas O'Shea's wealth and stature gave him standing in the community. Many feared him, for he could decide a man's fate with a flick of his pen. The banker held final decision making on many of the towns-people's property deeds and loans. His power and wealth made for an over-bearing countenance, being twice Deidre's age, he was determined to govern his new bride with the same domineering temperament he applied to his clients. Miss Doyle was just shy of her eighteenth birthday when the wedding took place. According to historical records, it was said to be quite the lavish affair. The young seamstress was a spirited girl, headstrong as she was beautiful. Her hazel eyes flecked with gold, while high cheekbones, and soft cupid-bow lips made for an angelic appearance. An hour-glass figure stirred the townsmen's imagination, and many took notice. But she was not just a pretty face. Along with her exquisite textile work and weaving skills, she was also a gifted artist.

"At first sight, the union appeared to be well-suited. In the beginning of their marriage, Mr. O'Shea showered his bride with expensive gifts, including a lavish trip abroad for their honeymoon. While away in Europe, he arranged carpenters to construct a lovely art room inside the large attic space on the second floor of Monarch Cove. After furnishing the room with an extensive collection of easels, paints, and canvases, the husband surprised his wife once they arrived home from overseas. The luxurious studio was said to be the envy of many creative souls in town. As I mentioned earlier, Carmel was a haven for artists and poets."

The realtor gazed out the dining room window, seemingly focused on the grounds below. As the room darkened, Jade sipped her tea and glanced over at Abby Dunsmuir. Startled, she studied the elderly woman's mottled complexion. A collection of spider-like veins stretched over her taut skin, and across her hallowed cheekbones. For just a moment, tiny capillaries appeared to pulsate beneath her ashen flesh.

What on earth? Jade thought to herself, closing her eyes briefly, trying to focus. When she opened them, the realtor was smiling, her pale eyes peering through coke-bottle sized lenses.

"Everything alright, Mrs. MacFie?"

Aidan glanced at his wife, and his smile faltered. "What's wrong, love?"

Jade suddenly realized she was staring, and quickly looked away. Feigning a smile, she sat back in her chair. "Oh, I'm sorry. Guess I was lost in the story. It's captured my imagination."

"Yes, I told you it would be fascinating," Abby said, reaching into her purse, searching for her cough drop tin. After popping a lozenge between her chapped lips, she folded her hands together and leaned back in her chair. The aroma of eucalyptus and stale tobacco intermingled.

Jade tried her best to ignore the sharp odor. It seemed there was another unpleasant scent lingering beneath. Trying to focus, she lifted her teacup to her lips. As she sipped her beverage, a torrent of rain washed over the bay windows.

Abby continued with her story. "Well, these days the art room is currently boarded over, but I imagine with some mild construction it would make a delightful studio or craft room."

Jade's brow raised. "Boarded over? That's odd."

The agent's smile slowly faded. "Well, apparently, there's a significant draft. These old mansions are expensive to heat, and the previous owner was known to be quite thrifty. But I'm sure it could be brought back to its original glory." The realtor turned her attention toward Jade. "Do you paint, young lady?"

"I don't." Jade glanced at Aidan, sensing Mrs. Dunsmuir was attempting to entice her into purchasing the house despite her sentiments otherwise.

"Well, according to sources, the husband was quite proud of his young bride's beauty and equally jealous of her admirers. To gain his wife's favors, he lavished the teenager with jewelry and expensive furs. Sadly, despite the husband having an affinity for gifting priceless treasures, he doled out discipline with equal intensity.

"One splendid summer afternoon, Deidre discovered the depths of her husband's controlling nature. After brunch, Mrs. O'Shea requested their driver to take her to town for a bit of shopping.

"Desiring to try out the couple's new ebony-colored barouche, Deidre instructed their groom to ready the horses for an excursion into town. The fancy, four-wheeled open carriage offered two double facing seats, along with a high outside box seat for the driver. Realizing Mr. O'Shea had taken the smaller buggy to the bank that day, Deidre decided to enjoy their new vehicle. Once their driver was ready, Mrs. O'Shea was escorted inside the airy interior and reclined gracefully against the ivory-colored seating. She enjoyed the fresh sea breeze as the dazzling pair of ebony thoroughbreds trotted toward Mainstreet. After they parked near the seaside, Deidre told her driver to take his lunch and prepare for her return before supper.

For several hours, Deidre explored the clothing boutiques and art galleries, spending extra attention to the seaside canvases displayed in the inviting gallery windows. After dropping off a hatbox with the driver, the young wife was ready to head home. Just as she was stepping up to take her seat, something unusual caught her eye. Across the road, along the white-sandy beach, was a collection of tents and campfires. Deidre asked her driver to wait while she took a closer look. With the warm August wind against her back, she moved toward the sparkling sea. Once she'd crossed the road, she noticed several paintings hanging on makeshift easels. Now, as I mentioned earlier, Carmel was, and remains, a beacon for artists and poets. Many creative souls had recently been displaced from the San Francisco Earthquake back in April. The mild temperature and scenic storybook charm of Carmel called them forth like moths to a flame," Abby said.

"How lovely. Reminds me of a scene from Jack London's novel, *Valley of the Moon*. Imagine all the talented artists and writers recently transplanted from San Francisco after the earthquake," Jade said.

"Indeed," Abby replied, continuing with her story.

As Mrs. Dunsmuir spoke, Jade listened in fascination, falling back in time as the sweet love story unfolded.

⚜

BENEATH QUIET CYPRESS TREES, DEIDRE O'SHEA NOTICED SEVERAL TENTS *surrounded by easels and cooking fires. She listened to overlapping conversations concerning art, literature, and poetry. Breathing in the aroma of abalone stew made her stomach rumble. Intrigued, she watched a dark-haired man stirring a fresh pot. Sunlight reflected his dark eyes while he offered a lopsided smile. Before she realized, the young bride moved toward his firepit. Turning to her right, she noticed an easel facing a tattered tent. A collection of upturned abalone shells propped together nearby. Glancing toward his canvas, she admired the still life drying in the summer sun. He'd captured the colors brilliantly, so lifelike in fact, it was difficult to determine reality from imagination.*

"Oh, your painting is quite lovely. Hope you don't mind my interruption," Deidre whispered.

"Hello, lass," he said, stirring a rusted pot swinging above simmering coals. "Of course, not. Glad ye like it. May I offer a bowl of abalone stew? Just finishing up right now. Supper's fresh," the stranger said, setting the ladle down on a tin plate." He reached his hand to hers. "Name's Johnathon."

She hesitated a moment before taking it. "Pleasure to meet you, Johnathon. I'm Deidre."

The young gentleman kissed the back of her gloved hand, keeping his brown eyes locked on her hazel ones. "Aye, that's a bonnie name. Please let me get ye something to sit upon," he said, rushing toward his canvas tent. He disappeared inside for a moment and emerged with a wooden crate. Turning it upside down, he gestured for her to have a seat.

"Sorry, miss. It's not much. We keep things simple around here."

"Thank you," Deidre said, shifting the bottom of her silk dress before sitting down. Her eyes wandered across the white sands, noticing several tents, along with a few wooden shelters.

"Ye seem curious about the neighborhood."

"Neighborhood?" Deidre asked, with her brows raised.

"Aye, our community is taking advantage of the dog days of summer. Why, it's an artist's paradise, so to speak. A bunch of us came down after the Frisco quake. My, what a time; what a time! Never seen so much destruction in my life. But we were lucky to find sanctuary in the lovely village of Carmel. Town folk been encouraging us ye might say. Rents cheap, and we've been treated more than fair."

"Oh, my. Sounds like a lovely adventure," she said, her hazel eyes shining.

Johnathon studied the young woman, his whiskey-brown eyes traveling over her lovely face and figure. After a particularly strong gust, the edge of her gown fluttered upward, exposing a flash of delicate ankle. The lad grinned, admiring her with a side-long glance. He moved back to his pot of stew and ladled a cupful into a tin bowl. She caught the glint of amber light in his beguiling eyes. They appeared flecked with stardust in the summer haze.

Taking a bite of the abalone stew, her eyes widened at the delicious flavor.

"Johnathon, this is absolutely divine!" She scooped up another spoonful, unaware of his admiring gaze.

He must think I'm famished, she thought, enjoying the satisfaction radiating from his handsome face.

"Glad ye enjoying the stew. A bunch of us go out diving in the early morning in search of the delicacies. God, I could live off the tasty meats for the rest of my life and be satisfied. Just another treasure from the glorious sea. Aye, it's a lovely place to be," he said, spooning up the rich stew from his tin bowl.

They sat in comfortable silence, enjoying their meal, while the wind carried its briny aroma. Seagulls plunged toward the breakers in search of sardines and plankton.

Time passed like a dream, the warmth of the afternoon sun caressing Deidre's fair skin, listening to the young man weave his stories of art and culture, offering a reprieve from her sheltered life at Monarch Cove. Before she realized, the hours passed in joyful banter. Forgetting her driver was waiting, and her husband would be arriving home from work any moment, she lost herself to the pleasure of the young man's company. With a fetching *brogue, he told his tale of coming to the States, an Irish immigrant, eventually making San Francisco his home. Soon after the quake, he carried his art supplies, a change of clothes, and little else, crossing by foot from the San Francisco Bay, and finally arriving to the white sandy beaches of Carmel. Deidre listened with fascination as the handsome youth spoke of the old country and his hopes of becoming an accomplished artist in America. The immigrant described his uncle, a wealthy gentleman who resided near 'the fancy side of town.'*

True wordsmiths by nature, the two artists soon found themselves immersed in lively conversations of art, culture, and poetry. When the August sun dipped below the horizon, the young bride reluctantly said her goodbyes, promising to visit again soon. While scarlet ribbons caressed the churning sea, Deidre reluctantly returned to the shadows of Monarch Cove.

🌸

JADE FOUND HERSELF LOST WITHIN THE TALE FROM LONG AGO, IMAGINING twilight's sheen mirroring the whiskey-colored eyes of the young artist, Johnathon, and the rosy blush of Deidre's cheeks. Surely the teen bride yearned for the company of creative souls like herself. As Abby Dunsmuir continued the story, a darker scene unfolded. Taking a sip of tea, the realtor continued her tale.

🌸

DEIDRE MOVED GRACEFULLY ACROSS THE MARBLE DINING ROOM FLOOR, TAKING her usual seat across from her husband. His smile didn't quite reach his mud-colored eyes, but she failed to notice. Thomas was unusually quiet as he listened to his young wife jabber on about her day.

Feeling encouraged by her husband's attentiveness, she spoke of her exciting excursion into town. How delightful the shops were, and the enticing aroma of jasmine kissing the summer air. In elaborate detail, Mrs. O'Shea described the town's enchantments, all the while Thomas O'Shea sipped his whisky, never losing eye contact. For nearly half an hour, she chatted away, eventually detailing meeting a talented group of artists by the beach. Deidre spoke of their spirited discussion of art, poetry, and the frightful events of the San Francisco earthquake. After mentioning her enthusiasm for the growing art community downtown, she shyly suggested they might host a party and invite the artists to their home.

Abby Dunsmuir leaned forward in her chair and gazed toward the bay windows.

"By the time Deidre finished her story, Mr. O'Shea had fallen into a blind rage. For not only had his young wife dared to leave their estate without permission, an unforgivable sin in his eyes, she'd flaunted herself, unescorted, amongst a seedy group of low-class artists and riffraff.

"I can only imagine the poor girl's terror. What happened next was a horrific scene. After knocking his chair backward, Thomas lunged toward his wife, slapping her violently across the face. Before Mrs. O'Shea fully realized what was happening, the banker was dragging her upstairs. Deidre's cries for help landed on deaf ears."

Jade shook her head. "How awful! Surely, someone could have intervened. Why didn't anyone help her?"

"I agree, Mrs. MacFie, but the world was a different place back then. And I imagine the servants feared losing their jobs if they dared interfere. As I mentioned earlier, Mr. Thomas O'Shea was a man of power and means. No one wanted to be on his bad side."

"Please go on. What happened next?" Jade asked, anxious for the conclusion of the tale.

"Well, as the story goes, Mr. O'Shea berated his wife with shameful accusations, calling her horrific names before locking her into the upstairs attic. With the slamming of the door, she found herself alone and bewildered. The once sunny art studio was now boarded over, only a thin beam of moonlight trickling through a tiny break in the knotty pine and slabs of driftwood. You see, her husband arrived in the early afternoon, eager to surprise his wife. When the servants explained she'd left for town, he became incensed. Not only was she late to supper, but she'd taken the brand-new barouche without his permission. While he waited for her to return, he hatched a sinister plan to punish his young bride.

"Mr. O'Shea entered his wife's studio with an armful of carpentry supplies. With a flickering smile, he approached her easel resting in front of the bay window. A lifelike portrait of their cat, Agatha, gazed back in the fading light. With pocketknife in hand, he plunged the steely tip into the drying canvas with abandon. After tossing the remains of her beloved portrait across the hardwood floor, he screamed for his staff to come upstairs. Once they were all in attendance, he instructed the shocked house-keepers to remove Deidre's remaining art supplies, easels, and canvases. After the attic was emptied, Thomas went to work boarding up the windows with slabs of oak and driftwood planks. Within the darkened room, the servants placed a moth-eaten mattress, a few raggedy quilts, and a rusty chamber pot against the far wall. After the changes were complete, the banker took his seat at the dining room table and waited. With each passing beat of the cuckoo clock, his anger mounted. By the time his wife arrived home that evening, he was full of whiskey and writhing with rage.

"Once imprisoned within the attic, the head housekeeper, Margaret, entered early in the morning to bring Mrs. O'Shea a small bowl of oatmeal and a pitcher of water. As far as emptying the chamber pot, Thomas insisted it be left alone. If Margaret failed to follow directions in any way, it would mean her job. Having four children and a disabled mother to care for guaranteed the housekeeper's silence.

"What an absolute monster," Jade whispered, horrified by the idea.

Abby nodded and continued. "After a week of isolation and humiliation, Deidre was finally released from her prison. Lady O'Shea was escorted from the attic by a young maid in attendance. According to first-hand witnesses, the Mistress of Monarch Cove appeared wildly disoriented. One can only imagine what she must have experienced during her stretch of solitude. Covering her eyes in the morning light, she was led to a hot bath. Afterward, she was instructed to change into a fresh summer gown. Her husband ordered a new wardrobe while his young bride languished in the dark. Once she was presentable, Deidre was escorted downstairs for breakfast. Terrified, she approached the dining room. Her husband gestured for her to take her usual place across from him. Once seated, Mr. O'Shea presented his wife with a large bouquet of roses, and a diamond brooch. Fearing for her life, she accepted the gifts without a word. In fact, Deidre would not speak again for several weeks." The agent placed her hands on the table with her fingers spread.

"It's simply monstrous!" Jade said, closing her eyes. "The poor woman. Sounds like her husband was a true psychopath. It's textbook abuse, punishment followed by gifts."

"Indeed, Mrs. MacFie. I agree. And sadly, Mr. O'Shea was only getting started."

Aidan squeezed Jade's hand.

The agent unwrapped another lozenge before continuing her story.

"While they ate their breakfast in silence, the staff prepared the attic. Once it was sanitized, they moved Deidre's art supplies back into the studio and removed the boards from the windows. Deidre fell into a deep depression after her harrowing imprisonment. She no longer dared leave the house without her husband chaperoning her. And she absolutely refused to set foot in the art studio. Traumatized, Lady O'Shea passed the time sitting on a wicker chair atop the back porch, listlessly staring at the seashore. Nearly a month went by before her husband decided it was time for his wife to snap out of it. He'd grown impatient by what he called Deidre's 'tiresome melancholia'," Abby said, making air quotes with her arthritic fingers.

"A few weeks later, Thomas escorted Deidre upstairs to the attic. Imagine she was terrified, but her husband insisted. Once inside, he instructed his wife to take her place by the easel and partake in her 'little hobby'. Fearing he'd punish her if she refused, she reluctantly obeyed. Listless, and nearly catatonic, her canvases took on darker themes and worrisome subject matter. Gone were her cheery portraits of beloved pets and delightful landscapes.

"Meanwhile, it was nearing autumn and many of Carmel's tourists were leaving town. However, numerous artists and writers stayed behind. As I mentioned earlier, the 1906 earthquake prompted creative souls to reestablish themselves in the sleepy seaside town. The previous year, the Carmel Arts and Crafts Club had formed. New residents were offered affordable housing, while many simply built wooden shelters and pitched tents along the shore. In fact, Jack London was often spotted by the beach, socializing, even cooking abalone stew. Such an incredible era," Abby said, leaning back in her chair.

"Wow! Imagine seeing Jack London hanging out at Carmel Beach! Sounds like paradise," Jade said.

"Yes. Carmel has always been a beacon for artists and free spirts," Mrs. Dunsmuir said, studying her porcelain teacup.

"On a breezy September afternoon, Mr. O'Shea instructed his wife to dress in a luxurious silver tea gown and wait for him in the parlor. The cypress trees surrounding the estate were just turning russet, and fall was on the horizon. Deidre waited listlessly, staring down at her gloved hands. When a young, dark-haired gentleman was ushered inside the parlor, her hazel eyes lit up. Stunned and speechless, she held her breath as her husband made introductions.

Mrs. Dunsmuir pushed a locket of silver hair behind her ear and smiled.

"It just so happened their guest was the young man Deidre met during her fateful excursion into town."

"The handsome artist?"

"Indeed. Now, Johnathon had spoken about his rich uncle when they were introduced, but he'd failed to mention his last name was O'Shea."

"O'Shea?" Jade asked with her mouth agape.

"Yes, Johnathon O'Shea was her husband's nephew. His eldest brother's, Gregory O'Shea's only son."

Aidan shook her head. "This is remarkable. Surely Mrs. O'Shea must have been shocked realizing Johnathon was related. What a strange coincidence."

"I agree, Mr. MacFie, but just wait. The story's about to take an intriguing turn." Abby Dunsmuir folded her sallow hands together and leaned forward.

"Deidre tried her best to contain her excitement when Thomas made formal introductions. After explaining his nephew, Johnathon O'Shea, was a recent transplant from Tipperary, Ireland, the uncle offered a tour of Monarch Cove. Deidre followed behind the men in shocked silence. During their walkabout, Thomas failed to mention his older brother, Gregory O'Shea, had inquired by letter several months prior. It was only after discovering his nephew could benefit him, did Thomas take the initiative to reach out. After locating his brother's son, Mr. O'Shea arranged for him to reside on the property for the next several months. The terms were simple. Johnathon would live in a modest shelter by the cove. Building material would be provided, but it would be his responsibility to construct a small cottage for himself. Luckily, the nephew was an accomplished carpenter as well as a talented painter. Interestingly, the entire O'Shea family were notable woodworkers. Might be the reason Thomas was able to effortlessly board up the attic windows the previous month before. But I digress," Abby said, sitting back in her chair.

"In exchange for free rent and board, Johnathon was commissioned to paint Lady O'Shea's official portrait."

Jade set her teacup back on the saucer. "Why didn't Mr. O'Shea allow his nephew to stay in the manor? He was family, after all."

"Well, as I've mentioned before, times were different back then. Mr. O'Shea disapproved of the arts as a proper, manly profession. And there was tension between the two brothers. Back in Tipperary, the eldest sibling, Gregory, was nearly destitute due to gambling debts. Years earlier, Thomas O'Shea abandoned their family carpentry business in order to seek his fortune in the States. Once he left, Gregory was unable to keep their century's old enterprise afloat, so he turned to less reputable ways of earning a living. It would be an understatement to suggest the O'Shea clan had a strained history. Thomas purposely ignored his brother's correspondences. And had no intention of helping his displaced nephew. It wasn't until he realized he could use the boy's talents did he contact Johnathon. And even then, his offer was far from generous. For he realized commissioning a professional portrait artist would have cost a pretty penny. But being it was his nephew; he negotiated the terms to his advantage.

"Once Johnathon learned of the portrait subject's identity, he was more than happy to oblige. Since their fateful meeting, Lady Deidre O'Shea was all he could think and dream about. It must have come as a complete shock when he discovered his uncle was in fact her husband. Despite the circumstances, they were equally infatuated with one another.

"During supper, Mr. O'Shea explained, to his speechless wife the fact that Johnathon would work on her portrait over the next couple of months while the weather permitted. Can you imagine the conversation?"

Jade shook her head. "I'm amazed he allowed her the opportunity. Her husband created such a fuss about her trip into town. Why was this any different?"

"Well, it's a good question. I have a few theories. Perhaps he believed his nephew was indeed harmless. But I've also wondered if this could have been a test. After all, he didn't require a chaperone during the sittings. Deidre and Johnathon spent the next couple of months as subject and artist unattended.

"Now, Mr. O'Shea had one stipulation, considering the portrait. He insisted his wife stand with her back to the cove to show off the seaside view of their estate. Other than that, Johnathon had complete artistic license. The young artist set up an easel near his cottage adjacent to the rocky cliffside. This made it easier for him to move the portrait inside when the weather was not cooperating. But as far as being alone and unchaperoned, who knows. I wouldn't be surprised if the husband had spies watching his nephew and wife, especially considering how the story ends."

Jade rested her palm on her cheek and groaned. "Oh, I'm afraid to ask. What happened?"

Before Abby continued, she leaned back in her chair, absently waving her hand at a horsefly buzzing near her face. Moments later, a second fly landed on the realtor's shoulder. And then a third. Jade watched the insects dart around the old woman in lackadaisical circles. Wondering where they were coming from, she glanced toward the kitchen window and gasped. Dozens of flies gathered behind the opaque glass, along with a collection of lifeless insects piled together near the bottom of the windowsill.

How bizarre, she thought to herself. Jade was certain the flies weren't there earlier. Before she could dwell on the fact, Abby continued with her story.

"Well, the next couple of months were paradise for Deidre and Johnathon. Mrs. O'Shea experienced unbridled freedom during the sittings. They chatted away the hours while the young artist captured his muse's vibrancy as the waves crashed along the rocky shore. Their love blossomed with each passing day. Interestingly, the nephew's cottage remains on the property to this day. It's behind the house overlooking the cliffside. Sadly, it's fallen to ruin over the years. Even so, the building weathered considerably well considering the harsh sea air."

Aidan folded his large hands together on the antique table. "Pardon my interrupting, Mrs. Dunsmuir, but why was Mr. O'Shea being so generous? Obviously, the bloke's an absolute bastard...pardon my language. Seems a bit odd considering his wife's previous circumstances he'd suddenly allow her independence. Doesn't make much sense."

"Good question. No one knows for sure, but I have my theories. Now, if you haven't guessed already, the portrait Johnathon painted is the one resting between the spiral staircases. Mr. O'Shea loved to show off his wealth and power. You see, he was a self-made man. Arrived in the States with nothing and created his own fortune. Now, the Irish were not well received in this country. Thomas tried his best to distance himself from his Celtic heritage. May have been another reason he took so long to reach out to his nephew. The husband wanted nothing to do with his meager beginnings, cutting all ties with relatives and old relations. His upcoming portrait unveiling was just another way to impress his neighbors. And after Deidre's trip to the seashore, he wasn't going to allow just any artist into his home. Perhaps he considered Johnathon a harmless boy. And as I mentioned before, the commission offered was meager in comparison to the young man's considerable talent," Abby said, reaching for the silver teapot. She stood from her chair and re-filled their porcelain cups. "I don't imagine Thomas O'Shea believed his wife would dare betray him after her last indiscretion."

Jade watched the steam rise from her rose-colored cup, steeling herself for the ending of the story.

"Now, I imagine artist and subject fell in love during their many sittings together. After all, they were both young, attractive, and shared a passion for the arts. And there was Johnathon's private cabin close by..." Mrs. Dunsmuir said with a wiggle of her penciled-in eyebrows.

Jade laughed, not expecting the innuendo.

"According to legend, the young lovers planned to run away together Christmas Eve. Johnathon finished the portrait in mid-December. Although his uncle allowed him to stay at the cabin, he explained his nephew's daily visits with Deidre were no longer necessary. Without an excuse to spend time with her lover, Mrs. O'Shea spent her leisurely moments working on her own art."

Jade folded her hands on her lap and leaned forward. "What was the subject matter?"

"Glad you asked. Interestingly, it was the seascape which disappeared during the estate sale. Believed to have been her last known work."

Jade released her breath, trying to remain calm as she put together the missing pieces of the puzzle. *Was Deidre O'Shea's final painting the phantom portrait? Was she using her artwork to communicate with the living? If so, she needed Madame Garnier's opinion on the matter. Perhaps they could figure out the mystery together.* A gnawing suspicion suggested Deidre O'Shea was indeed the Grey Lady of Monarch Cove.

Abby leaned forward. "Imagine time passed slowly for Deidre once her official portrait was completed. Perhaps painting distracted her during her lonely hours waiting for the day she could escape with her lover."

"But how did she plan to do it? Surely, she must have been terrified of being caught?" Jade said, studying Mrs. Dunsmuir's profile in the darkening room.

A sharp crack of thunder erupted overhead. Drops of rain rolled down the kitchen window, blurring the scenery outside before washing away the collection of flies crawling over the glass. In the distance, a buzzing sound pulsated. Unable to determine the source, Jade turned her attention back to Mrs. Dunsmuir, her grey eyes settling on her narrow face. A plump fly landed atop her translucent cheek. Flicking its brown-veined wings, it crawled downward toward the hollow of her throat. Trying not to stare, Jade took a sip of tea, glancing over the rim of her cup. After the insect disappeared, a purplish mound of scar tissue swelled above the agent's starched collar.

What is going on? Where were all the flies coming from? she asked herself, suddenly wanting to flee the strange estate. That awful scar wasn't there a minute ago, she thought, feeling her reality beginning to crumble. She closed her eyes, trying not to panic. After she opened them, everything appeared back to normal. The realtor's throat lacked any trace of injury. Jade glanced at Aidan, who appeared unaware of anything out of the ordinary. Taking a deep breath, she listened to the remainder of the agent's ghost story.

"Christmas Eve arrived on a dark December day. Despite the gloomy weather, Monarch Cove was alive with Christmas cheer and festivities. The wealthiest and most noteworthy people in town were invited to the lavish affair. The holly-covered halls were packed with guests, eagerly waiting the grand unveiling. The portrait was hung where it remains today, covered in a scarlet-covered velvet cloth."

Once again, Jade's mind swept back to 1906, imagining the wealth and grandeur of the O'Shea's Christmas Eve party.

෮෴෬

WHILE THE GUESTS ENJOYED APPETIZERS AND FLUTES OF CHAMPAGNE, DEIDRE tried her best to be a gracious hostess. Mingling with the well-dressed ladies and gentlemen, her mind kept drifting back to Johnathon and their planned escape. She searched the throng of guests, noting her lover's absence. Where could he be? she wondered. Moving through the circling women showing off their luxurious Edwardian gowns and dainty bonnets from Paris, Mrs. O'Shea entertained and made small talk.

With the ringing of a golden bell, the group was escorted to the dining hall at six o'clock sharp. Mr. and Mrs. O'Shea took their regular seats across from one another. They enjoyed a lavish goose supper with all the trimmings. Halfway through the meal, Deidre glanced up, noticing her husband grinning ear-to-ear. His smile did not reach his dark eyes. A wave of apprehension coursed through her body. Once the spirited guests finished with their dessert, they were offered brandy and Champagne and escorted back to the velvet-covered portrait hanging between the spiraling staircases. Mr. O'Shea reached for his wife's hand while the servants pulled back the crimson ropes. When the portrait was revealed, the party goers gasped their appreciation and expressed admiration for the artwork. Deidre's husband smiled at his wife. In a voice just above a whisper, Mrs. O'Shea asked the question, "Where is Johnathon? I'm sure he would enjoy everyone's appreciation for his work."

Mr. O'Shea offered a tight smile. "Appears the lad hasn't showed up for the party tonight."

When she heard the news, Deidre's stomach clenched. Stepping closer to his wife, her husband whispered in her ear. "Why so sad, little wife? Surely you don't miss him already?"

Sensing Thomas was toying with her, she moved backward. He tightened his hand on her wrist, pulling her close to his chest. Deidre tried to hide her revulsion as the sharp aroma of whiskey wafted from his gaping mouth.

"What's wrong, love? Were you looking forward to spending time with your special friend?" Before she could answer, her husband continued. "Guess the apple doesn't fall far from the tree. Seems like my nephew is as irresponsible as his father." He chuckled, glaring into her hazel eyes.

"But don't worry, darlin'. You can spend time with me tonight. Save some room on your dance card, won't ye?"

Mr. O'Shea reached for her gloved hand. Peeling back the satin until her bare skin showed, he pressed his lips to her palm, at once sending an icy shiver coursing through her body.

"After our guests leave, we'll enjoy a special romantic evening together. And make no mistake, I plan to enjoy every inch of my wife's lovely enchantment," he said, his muddy eyes boring into her. "For now, I suggest you remove that pouty expression and entertain our guests. Don't disappoint, Lady O'Shea. Do you understand me?" he asked, squeezing her hand painfully before releasing it.

Forcing a smile, while blinking back hot tears, she nodded. "Yes, darling. I won't disappoint you."

Smirking, her husband disappeared into the throng of guests. Once he was gone, Deidre turned her attention toward a group of middle-aged ladies admiring the portrait. The hours trickled by painfully slow, and all the while she hoped and waited for Johnathon to appear and ease her troubled mind.

While she engaged an endless line of wealthy women, talking the latest fashion trends of Europe and listening to an array of sordid town gossip, her mind wandered back to her midnight rendezvous. Deidre's stomach tightened, noticing her husband watching her from across the room, bourbon in hand. Something was wrong and she could feel it. Where was Johnathon? If she could only gaze into his whiskey-brown eyes, listen to him explain everything was going to be alright. She yearned for his touch, his gentle embrace. Perhaps he was at his cabin now, getting ready for her. Yes, that was it. He just needed a little more time to prepare. She couldn't entertain any other possibilities. For if she did, Deidre feared her reality would shatter, sending her into an abyss of utter madness. Tonight, was her final chance at freedom.

Knowing Mr. O'Shea enjoyed his bourbon to excess, Deidre waited for the alcohol to take effect. When she was certain he was distracted, she took her opportunity and dashed upstairs. Making sure no one noticed her; she slipped inside the master bedroom and locked the door. After retrieving a small satchel from beneath the bed, she pulled a heavy coat from the wardrobe and opened their balcony window. The evening was dark and cold, which worked to her advantage. The backyard was absent of guests, so she pulled a kerosene lamp from beneath the dresser and made her way onto the terrace below. A metal stairway connected the second-floor landing. Despite the darkness, and slippery surface, she managed her way down the side of the building. According to the plan, Johnathon set a ladder earlier that day beneath the bougainvillea, camouflaging her escape. With this new addition, she was able to climb the rest of the way down to the garden level.

When she was a safe distance from the house, Mrs. O'Shea lit her kerosene lamp and headed toward her lover's cabin. Anxiously, she remembered Johnathon's instructions. They would ride together to the boating dock. The young lovers would board a ship destined to Johnathon's home-

town of Tipperary, Ireland. Once they were on the open seas, they would finally be free from the clutches of Thomas O'Shea. Deidre glanced down at the velvet satchel in her gloved hand, thinking of its contents. All the jewelry her husband had ever gifted her was stashed inside. She would sell the entire collection when they reached the Emerald Isle, far away from the dark memories of Monarch Cove. Her body trembled as she reached the final yards leading to the wooden building. So many wonderful memories were created behind closed doors. In Johnathon's powerful arms, she'd blossomed in love and desire. She swung the light toward the churning sea, illuminated the powerful breakers below. Beneath the starless sky, the ground was particularly treacherous, and she was cautious to avoid the slippery boulders along the shore. When she finally made it to the threshold, she released her breath.

The door was ajar.

Trembling, she pushed the barrier open, but her lover was nowhere to be found. Not one trace of his belongings remained. With her heart pounding in her ears, she turned back to the shore, calling his name in vain. As the minutes turned to hours, Deidre was left to pick up the pieces of her shattered dreams.

۞

AS THE STORMY WEATHER CONTINUED, SHEETS OF RAIN SWEPT OVER Monarch Cove while gnarled branches scraped the mansion's stained-glass windows. All the while the sound of a ticking cuckoo clock counted down the minutes.

Jade shook her head, slowly coming back to reality.

"What a heartbreaking story. Do you believe Johnathon abandoned her? Did her husband discover their plan? What happened to Deidre O'Shea?" She leaned forward, desperate for answers.

Abby smoothed the starched collar from her canary yellow blazer and reached for another lozenge from her purse. While popping a stale cough drop between chapped lips, a botfly landed on her ashen cheek. Absently swatting it away with her fingers, she continued with the story. For a moment, Jade tuned out the woman's voice, concentrating instead on a distant humming. It was difficult to determine the source of the noise beneath the sound of wind and rain. At times, it appeared to be coming from down the hallway, and other instances, near the ceiling. Then it would disappear altogether. Something was wrong, that was certain. Jade glanced toward her husband who was listening attentively to Mrs. Dunsmuir. He appeared unaware that anything was out of the ordinary. She glanced over his shoulder toward the kitchen window. Once again, the glass was crawling with insects. With horror, she realized they were now inside the house, moving in frantic circles against the blurry glass. Trying her best not to panic, Jade folded her hands on the table, trying to ground herself.

Why isn't anyone paying attention? And where are the flies coming from? Mixed with the scent of eucalyptus and stale cigarettes, another odor surfaced. The putrid scent was a nauseating combination of rotting fruit, rancid and warm.

Surely, I'm not the only one aware? Jade thought, gazing at her husband. Aidan rested his head on the back of his right hand, apparently engrossed by Mrs. Dunsmuir's tale.

Abby continued talking, seemingly oblivious of anything out of the ordinary. Twisting her wedding ring, Jade tried to rein in the bright embers of panic welling inside. Instead, she focused on the sound of the elderly woman's gravelly voice.

"Some believe Deidre slipped on the rocks and fell to her death, lost to the churning tides of the Pacific. Mrs. O'Shea was not seen again after the night of the Christmas Eve party. Her husband reported her missing Christmas morning. Although there was a formal investigation, and suspicions around the disappearance, the police did not pursue her husband as a suspect."

"Why not?" Jade asked.

"As I mentioned before, Mr. O'Shea was a powerful man with money and means. The townspeople feared him, and he had plenty of ways to pay off the police. And if that didn't work, the mere threat of his displeasure was enough. You see, he could determine a man's fate with the flick of his pen. It was a developing town in 1906; people needed loans for housing. Fearing retaliation, the sheriff let the matter pass."

"What was Thomas's next move?" Aidan asked, his brow furrowing.

Jade noticed her husband was just as intrigued by the story as she was. Abby turned her head slightly, looking past him.

"It's a bit of a mystery. For the next couple of weeks, pallets of wood and carpentry supplies were delivered to Monarch Cove. Soon after, construction began, bringing with it endless nights of hammering and sawing. But strangely, no workmen were ever seen coming or going from the estate. And the widowed banker didn't volunteer any information. And then one stormy evening, the construction noises stopped altogether. Imagine the neighbors were quite relieved when they finally regained their peace and quiet.

"For Mr. O'Shea's part, he played up the grieving widow to his advantage. Neighborhood women brought him home-cooked meals and checked in on him often, offering words of encouragement and advice. According to town gossip, a few ladies offered much more. After all, Thomas O'Shea was one of the wealthiest men in town. It did not take him long to file for Deidre's petition of death certificate. The official conclusion, although the body was never recovered, determined Mrs. O'Shea slipped and fell to her death Christmas Eve. She was lost to the treacherous sea. If anyone doubted her fate, no one came forward.

"One year to the day of her disappearance, Thomas O'Shea announced his marriage to his second wife, Lady Elizabeth Beaumont. The young debutant came from a well-to-do family tied to the shipping trade. Her father was greatly known in the sardine markets, and heavily invested in Cannery Row. Once the blushing bride took the title of the new Mrs. O'Shea, she wasted no time in placing her unique stamp upon Monarch Cove. She hired movers and designers and the estate soon took on a European flare. Embracing the French Provincial style, the manor boasted gold leaf benches and armrests, damask, and opulent crystal chandeliers.

"In the beginning of their marriage, Thomas O'Shea humored his new wife. But when she attempted to have Lady O'Shea's portrait removed from the staircase, Mr. O'Shea flew into a violent rage and the subject was never broached again. The couple remained married for another ten years before his second wife succumbed to cirrhosis of the liver. It was rumored that she drank to excess near the end of her life, possibly in response to her husband's erratic behavior, and frequently reported manic episodes. Those closest to the couple believed it was a blessing their union failed to produce any children. After Lady Elizabeth's death, Mr. O'Shea appeared agitated and confused, especially in the evenings when he partook in excessive amounts of bourbon. Day drinking followed soon after. He eventually took to skipping time at the bank, refusing to leave the grounds of Monarch Cove. Thomas had trouble keeping on staff, his housekeepers had grown weary of his frequent outbursts. According to first-hand accounts, the middle-aged widow spent many evenings standing beneath Deidre's portrait subdued, seemingly catatonic. Other times he would scream and curse at the canvas. He eventually became a recluse, firing his remaining servants and refusing to leave the house all together. He died just shy of his fifty-third birthday, succumbing to a massive coronary event directly beneath Lady O'Shea's infamous portrait. Some say the O'Shea's never left, that their spirits still roam the halls of Monarch Cove."

"Do you believe it's haunted?" Jade asked.

Abby Dunsmuir sucked on a cough drop, cocking her head to the side.

"Well, I believe some spirits don't realize they've passed. When this happens, their souls linger. And others simply want to stay! Can you imagine abandoning such a beautiful home as Monarch Cove?" Abby asked, gazing toward the bay window buzzing with flies.

Astonished, Jade noted their appearance had little effect on the elderly woman.

With the darkening of storm clouds, the rancid odor of spoiled meat infiltrated the breakfast nook. Glancing at her husband in alarm, Jade fidgeted with the napkin on her lap. Despite the bizarre situation, Aidan's face appeared relaxed and untroubled. Before she could ask if he noticed anything unusual, the sound of Abby's gravelly voice broke through her strange musings.

"Well, my goodness. I'm afraid I took up most of your lovely afternoon," Mrs. Dunsmuir said, standing from her chair. Jade held her breath, trying to ignore the overwhelming aroma of decay. Aidan pulled out Jade's seat before squeezing her hand. Jade locked eyes with her husband, trying to communicate without words. His brow rose in confusion, unaware of his wife's uneasiness.

"I'm going out for a little smoking break, dearies." The realtor gathered her cup and saucer before heading toward the kitchen. "It was a pleasure having your company today. Does get a bit lonely at times. As my mother used to say, 'old age ain't for sissies'. Please feel free to explore Monarch Cove to your heart's content. I'll be out back if you have any questions."

As the agent turned to leave, Jade offered to help carry the remaining dishes.

"Thank you, dear. You can just set them down in the sink. I'll clean up after my smokes," Abby said, flashing a yellow-toothed grin. As she smiled, chartreuse-colored veins stretched across her forehead.

"Mrs. Dunsmuir, are you feeling alright?"

"Why, of course! Couldn't be better. Why do you ask?"

Jade stumbled for an answer, trying to explain without offending. Her words failed her, so she feigned a smile instead.

"Oh, I just wanted to make sure you were okay."

"How sweet. Rest assured, I'm simply marvelous. Well, now, I'll be outside if you need anything," she said, pushing her bifocals to the bridge of her narrow nose. As she turned to leave, Abby succumbed to a powerful coughing fit, and her face took on an alarming shade of crimson.

Struggling to catch her breath, her pale eyes filled with tears.

"Darn cigarettes. Oh, my, they're going to be the end of me one day. Never take up the habit, young lady. They're murder to quit!"

Unsettled, Jade listened to the old woman suck in a shallow breath, the sound of raspy phlegm thick and unyielding. And then, with dismay, she noticed a second cluster of blue-green veins spread over Mrs. Dunsmuir's slender neck. The heady scar reappeared on Abby's throat, before spreading toward her jawline. Spiderlike capillaries snaked upwards, reminding Jade of the trailing vines covering the backyard of her cottage.

"Are you alright, Mrs. Dunsmuir?" Jade cried, rushing to her side.

Abby shook her head, waving her away. Absently retrieving another lozenge, she pushed it between tarnished teeth.

"No, I'm fine. Don't trouble yourself." As color rushed back to her mottled face, she smoothed the collar of her canary yellow blazer.

Lowering her voice to a whisper, Abby took Jade's hands in hers.

"Please keep in touch, Mrs. MacFie." Jade instinctively pulled back, feeling frigid flesh against her own.

"I think we'll be seeing one another sooner than you realize," Mrs. Dunsmuir said.

"Oh?" Jade asked, trying not to grimace.

"Just a hunch, young lady. But what does a silly old woman like me know?" she asked with a wink. Waving an age-spot covered hand over her shoulder, the agent turned on her heel, making her way down the darkened hallway.

Stunned, Jade watched the realtor shuffle across the marble-floored corridor, disappearing into the shadows.

❦

ONCE ABBY DUNSMUIR WAS GONE, JADE HURRIED BACK TO AIDAN. Dougal was curled up against his boots, fast asleep.

"Oh, my God! Aidan, have you ever seen anything like it in your life? That poor woman. What on earth is going on with all the flies? And that horrible odor?"

Her husband's brows drew together as he studied his wife's startled face. Shrugging his broad shoulders, he stood from his chair. "Sorry, love, but what are you talking about?"

Jade's mouth gaped. "Are you kidding me? There are flies all over the kitchen window, for God's sake! Didn't you see them crawling all over Abby Dunsmuir?" Aidan followed his wife into the kitchen for a better look.

"What flies?"

Jade stared in disbelief. Raindrops rolled across the bay windows, washing away damp leaves and debris clinging to the glass; but there wasn't a hint of insects, dead or alive.

"I don't understand. There were dozens of flies just a minute ago. You must have seen them swarming. And that poor old woman. They kept landing on her face and neck. God, I didn't notice at first, but she has a terrible scar on her throat. Maybe from a tracheotomy? I'm not sure. Of course, I didn't ask." Jade wrung her hands, looking over her shoulder to make sure they were alone. "Not to mention the terrible odor," she whispered, scrunching up her face.

"The cigarettes, you mean. Figured it must have been bothering you. Ye seemed uncomfortable."

"Well, yes, the cigarettes and cough drops smelled awful, but there's something much worse lingering beneath. Seemed to get stronger right before she left. It was positively putrid. Ugh." Jade said, pursing her lips. She stepped toward the kitchen window, feeling off balance.

"It's not too bad right now, but a few minutes ago, honestly, I thought I was going to be sick. I don't know. It's an old house, so maybe there's something wrong with the plumbing?" She trailed off, realizing her husband was staring at her.

"You don't smell it, do you?" Jade asked, tears welling in her eyes.

Aidan moved closer. "Afraid not, love."

Jade was quiet for almost an entire minute, trying to gather her thoughts.

Aidan placed his hands on his wife's shoulders and kissed her forehead.

"Just because I didn't notice anything unusual doesn't mean I don't believe you. Do you suppose you might be getting one of your visions again? After all, this house seems to have a sordid history. Maybe you're picking up on something supernatural?"

Jade shook her head in frustration. "I don't know. This whole afternoon has given me the creeps. It's one thing to dream about future events. Having visions while awake is just too much."

"Maybe we should just leave. Honestly, you don't look like you feel well."

Although Aidan's offer sounded inviting, she wasn't ready to vacate the property just yet.

"Let's take a look upstairs. Just a feeling. Believe me, I don't want to stay in this house another minute longer than necessary. But Abby mentioned Lady O'Shea's final painting. It was an ocean scene; and I couldn't help but wonder if she might be speaking of the phantom portrait above our fireplace. After all, we never found out where it came from. It's an odd coincidence the artwork surfaced when I was sorting boxes from the Monarch Cove estate sale back in October. If Deidre died tragically, and I feel she probably did, perhaps she's reaching out in some way," Jade said.

Listening to the willow branches scratch the skylight above, she turned toward her husband and smiled. "Do you mind taking a quick peek?"

"Of course not."

Jade's brow rose. "Where's Dougal?"

Aidan walked toward the kitchen table.

"Dougal? Where did you go, boy?" He turned toward his wife. "Maybe exploring?"

"Maybe. He seemed spooked since we arrived. Surprised he left on his own."

"Well, let's take a look upstairs."

Aidan took his wife by the elbow, and they headed toward the staircase. When the couple glanced at Deidre O'Shea's portrait, the cuckoo clocked chimed from down the hall.

"What ye thinking?" Aidan asked, his dark brows pulling together.

"I'm not sure. There's something wrong with this house. And it's not just relating to the story we just heard. There are just too many coincidences. Earlier this week, Madame Garnier visited the shop. She mentioned energies sometimes attach themselves to everyday items. We also discussed her psychic abilities…and possibly mine."

Aidan took Jade's hand and gazed into her grey eyes. "Well, she did imply you had some special gifts the night at the cottage." Leaning close, he whispered, "Go ahead, love. You can tell me the rest if you're comfortable."

"Thank you." Jade chewed her lower lip, trying to keep her voice steady as they climbed the stairs. "Madame Garnier believes I may have connections to the other side of the veil. Although it's the last thing I really want right now, she believes spirits may be drawn to me."

"Spirits? Like ghosts?" Aidan asked.

"I guess." Jade hesitated, fearing what she prepared to say out loud. "What if the portrait and photograph have somehow summoned the Grey Lady's spirit? I know it sounds crazy, but I'm sensing Deidre O'Shea is not at rest. Could she be reaching out?"

"Aye, that's a troubling thought. If so, what do you suppose she wants?"

Jade shook her head. "During Friday's dinner, Madame Garnier reacted terribly to both the photograph and portrait. It was obvious she was troubled when she left that night. And, of course, the channeling of the young woman was incredibly unsettling. I knew she was psychic, but our friend also appears to be a powerful medium. The way her appearance changed was shocking. We need to find exactly who or what Madame Garnier was contacting Friday night. Looking forward to discussing our visit today; perhaps it's all connected. Love to hear her thoughts." Jade stopped in mid-sentence, listening to a pulsing sound echoing from the second floor.

"What is that?" Aidan asked.

"Let's take a closer look," Jade said.

Once they reached the top of the spiraling staircase, they followed a dark hallway covered by framed photographs, several dating back to the early nineteenth century. Most of the rooms were closed, except for the master bedroom. The sounds of the couple's footsteps echoed down the hallway as they moved toward the open door. Pausing by the entrance, they considered the luxurious bedroom with oceanfront views. Across from a king-sized bed was an antique fireplace with a golden-framed seascape above the mantel. Upon entering, they moved toward the painting.

Jade's eyes narrowed when she studied the canvas.

"I wonder if this could be the cove by their home. The one where Mrs. O'Shea intended to meet her lover that fateful night? Perhaps painted by Deidre herself? It's similar in style to the one at our cottage. Only difference is the lack of figures."

Aidan nodded. "Aye, you're correct. I see the similarity. Interesting."

As he said this, an icy wind fluttered the lace curtains. A French provincial vanity sat in the corner of the room, and Jade considered the antique furniture.

"This estate presents like a museum. The master bedroom set dates between the late eighteenth to early 19th century. Quite valuable. Interesting how many precious antiques were left behind. Perhaps the previous home-owners were superstitious about moving them. Makes sense, considering the lore surrounding Deidre O'Shea's portrait. I wonder if this trickled over to some of her personal items. Hope we haven't unleashed something by receiving possessions from the estate sale. If so, I'd be happy to return them...."

She stopped in mid-sentence as a high-pitched howl sounded from down the hallway.

"Dougal?" Jade whispered, glancing at her husband.

Rushing toward the frantic cries, they discovered their terrier scratching and clawing a mahogany door at the end of the hall. Despite his insistence, the Scottie could not penetrate the heavy boards.

"Come here, boy," Aidan said. With his stubby tail between his legs, the dog reluctantly obeyed his master's command. While Jade consoled the frightened pet, her husband took a closer look at the door.

"Do ye suppose this might be the attic Abby Dunsmuir was talking about? Mentioned it was boarded over," he said, glancing over his shoulder. Jade walked closer, inspecting the odd configuration. When she moved her fingers over the wood, the planks appeared porous.

"Resembles driftwood from the beach," Jade said, eyeing the uneven slabs.

"Odd choice," Aidan said.

Biting her lower lip, she listened to the buzzing sound coming from inside the room.

"This must be the attic where poor Deidre was locked away," Jade said.

Relying on instinct, she closed her eyes before reaching for the crystal doorknob. In an instant, she found herself transported into the dank chamber, staring at the opposite side of the door.

"Aidan!" Jade screamed. Hearing Dougal's high-pitched cries, she pounded her small fists against the partition. Anguished sobbing sounded from the back of the attic, and she spun on her heel. Squinting into the darkness, she noticed a trickle of light penetrating a collection of oak boards covering a bay window. With trembling hands, she fumbled with her purse, searching for her cellphone. With a sigh of relief, she clicked the flashlight app and moved the phone in a wide circle, illuminating her surroundings. Tentatively, she moved across the room, being careful to avoid the soiled mattress and bedpan set in the righthand corner. She put her hand to her nose, trying to ward off the unpleasant aroma of mold and decay. A pulsing sound vibrated overhead as tiny beads of light formed across the unkempt bed. As the noise strengthened, the bright form of a woman solidified. Tangled waves of brunette locks fell around the apparition's slender shoulders. Weeping and moaning, the ghostly form pressed its back against the wall. As Jade stared helplessly into the woman's anguished hazel eyes, the haunting blast of a foghorn bleated. Simultaneously, she found herself on the opposite side of the door, with Aidan and Dougal by her side.

The terrier whimpered while her husband gazed down at her bewildered face.

"What's wrong, love? You look like you've seen a ghost."

Unconceivable terror enveloped her like a cocoon when she realized the veils of life and death were thinning. Even more troubling was the fact that Aidan was oblivious to what had just taken place.

Pushing a locket of golden hair from his wife's forehead, Aidan studied Jade in the dim light. Taking her hand in his, he leaned close. "Your fingers feel like they've been submerged in ice water, and you're pale as a sheet. What's going on?" He kissed her forehead as she pressed herself against him.

Jade lowered her voice. "There's something terrible happening inside the attic. We both noticed a buzzing sound earlier, so I was curious if it was coming from inside the boarded room. Once I touched the doorknob, I found myself inside the old art studio. Heard Dougal's crying on the other side, but when I called out to you, there was no answer. Didn't you hear me?"

Aidan bit the corner of his lip and shook his head.

"Darlin', you never left my side. Not sure what you're talking about. Think we need to get ye some fresh air. If this mystery is over a century old, we'll need time to solve it. Let's go, love."

Jade released her breath as Aidan escorted her downstairs. With each passing step, she felt a sense of relief. She couldn't get far enough away from the dismal attic space and the terrible sobbing emanating from the decaying walls. Just as they were leaving the parlor, Jade glanced at her husband.

"Maybe we should say goodbye to Mrs. Dunsmuir."

Reluctantly, they headed back to the kitchen. After seeing it was empty, the couple glanced out the bay window. After a few minutes of searching, they decided to leave.

"That's odd," Jade said. "I wonder where she went?"

"Perhaps another smoking break?" Aidan said, wiggling his eyebrows.

"Wouldn't surprise me. Well, I guess we can just leave a message on her cellphone to thank her for the information."

"Good idea, lass."

Once they stepped out onto the front steps of the mansion, Jade released her pent-up breath. The heavy atmosphere immediately lifted. Even the air seemed lighter, cleaner. With the December sun breaking through the cloud barrier, they headed to the SUV. Dougal pulled on his tether, eager to leave the property.

For the next couple of hours, they walked along Main Street, enjoying the tourist shops and art galleries. By the early evening, they were famished and decided to visit an indoor pub. Just as the waiter set their drinks on the table, Aidan's phone rang, and he looked down with his brows raised.

"Hello, this is Aidan MacFie."

"Hello, Mr. MacFie. This is Helen Connor. I'm so sorry I couldn't make it for our appointment today. I understand you were interested in a viewing of Monarch Cove. Had a bit of a family emergency, but everything is handled now. Tried to call you earlier to leave a message but wasn't able. Your number went straight to voicemail. Perhaps your inbox is full. Anyway, if you're still interested in viewing the property, I have some time on Sunday."

"Oh, that's perfectly fine. Sorry to hear about your family emergency. Not sure what's going on with my phone. Didn't even hear it ring.

Concerning the showing, thank you, but we already met with another agent this afternoon."

"Really? Do you mind sharing the realtor's name? Didn't realize there was a viewing scheduled today. I'm the listing agent, and I'm usually informed beforehand."

"Of course. Abby Dunsmuir met with us this afternoon. We really enjoyed meeting her and touring Monarch Cove. She appeared quite knowledgeable concerning both the property and history of the area."

Nearly a minute of silence stretched before the agent responded.

"Hello, are you still there?" Aidan asked.

In a voice just above a whisper, the realtor answered.

"I think you're mistaken, sir. Abby Dunsmuir *was* an agent with our company, but that was several years ago."

"Was?" Aidan asked, his brow furrowing.

"Yes, Mrs. Dunsmuir passed away last summer. She managed our firm back when I was a new hire. Interestingly, she was also the previous owner of Monarch Cove. Lovely woman. I was quite sad to hear of her passing, but was truly amazed she lived so long with her terrible smoking habit. Eventually needed a tracheotomy just to breathe. Poor thing succumbed to late-stage Alzheimer's at the ripe old age of eighty-five. Kept to herself the last few years, even gave up volunteering at the Historical Society. Sad really. Became a recluse in the end, never wanted to leave the estate. Anyway, whoever showed you the property couldn't possibly be Abby Dunsmuir. Unless, of course, you met with her ghost," she said with a nervous chuckle.

Aidan stood gaping at the phone.

"May I get back to you?"

"Of course. If I don't answer, just leave a message. I'll be working in Carmel all day Sunday."

"Thank you," Aidan said, clicking off his cell.

"Is everything all right?" Jade asked, noticing her husband's concerned expression.

He shook his head and sat back in his seat. "Well, if what the agent just told me is correct, we apparently had tea with a ghost."

Chapter Eight

AIDAN RELAYED THE PHONE CONVERSATION WHILE JADE LISTENED speechless. Minds racing, the newlyweds paid for their meal and headed home to Pacific Grove. Dougal curled between his owners, sensing their unease. Despite the bizarre realization they'd seemingly met spirits during their visit to Monarch Cove, neither one wanted to be the first to broach the unsettling topic. They found solace in knowing whatever happened, they'd face it together. After their spooky adventure, they enjoyed comfort in each other's arms the remainder of the weekend. Their lovemaking was passionate, as their unearthly encounter made them both aware that life was finite. Every second was a gift not to be wasted.

With Aidan called to work for the next two days, Jade focused on working at the shop and caring for their pets. After spending an hour at a local nursery, she selected two potted Douglas fir trees. Balancing one of the potted trees in her arms, she maneuvered her new focal piece in front of the store by the bay window. Once the tree was in place, Dougal sniffed the branches with interest.

"Please don't get any ideas, buddy," Jade said with a smile.

After his examination was complete, the terrier trotted back to his bed by the window and plopped down with a heavy sigh.

"Good boy." Jade reached inside her pocket, searching for a doggie treat. She placed the rawhide stick on Dougal's plaid blanket, and he went to work chewing his prize. As she fetched a box of ornaments from the back room, Morrigan flew from her perch. With a streak of ivory feathers, she landed on the top branch of the evergreen.

"You guys are too much," she said, shaking her head.

"Are you going to be our Christmas angel?" Jade asked, studying the raven with amusement.

Morrigan stretched her wings against the conifer branches. With the tangy scent of pine needles filling the room, Jade turned her attention toward a tote of vintage Christmas ornaments stored by the cash register. She clicked on the radio and nostalgic Christmas music filled the shop. Humming along to Nat King Cole, Jade went to work organizing a collection of holiday treasures. Despite the festive atmosphere, her mind drifted back to Deidre O'Shea.

"God, that poor woman," she whispered to herself, shivering in the drafty room. After turning on the heater, Jade tried focusing on work, slipping a gold foiled ornament over the end of a conifer branch. Morrigan ruffled her feathers, soft blue eyes locked with Jade's grey ones.

"Sorry, sweet girl. I didn't mean to disturb you."

When the ivory raven cawed, Jade laughed and reached for another vintage ornament. By the time she was finished decorating, long shadows stretched across the stone floors. Folding her arms over her chest, she gripped her shoulders and examined her handiwork. Satisfied with the handsome-looking display, her attention was suddenly drawn toward the front window. Garnet rays spilled through onyx clouds, sending bands of crimson radiance across the tree-lined sidewalk. Within moments, twilight's ephemeral glow settled onto the quiet neighborhood. Watching the heavy cypress boughs bending in the wind, Jade sipped her coffee. With a grimace, she set down the paper cup on the mahogany table, realizing the contents had grown cold and bitter. Turning her attention back to Lighthouse Avenue, she noticed a light rain peppering the tourists rushing by with their umbrellas. Realizing foot traffic was fizzling, she turned the shop's open sign to closed and bolted the door. For the next half hour, she broke down boxes and totaled her receipts at the register. Despite the newly achieved holiday atmosphere, the troubling visit to Carmel-by-the-Sea was fresh in her mind. The endless loop of haunting images, and imagined horrors, pressed on her nerves. Trying her best not to dwell on the story, she decided to act. If this meant endless hours reading online articles and poring over countless books about Monarch Cove, so be it. At least she would be doing something constructive to solve the grey lady mystery. Listening to the distant boom of thunder, she hurried through her final receipts and called it a night.

Once her pets were loaded inside the truck, she leaned against the driver's seat and flicked on the heat. As she headed down Lighthouse Avenue, the truck's windshield wipers sliced through layers of heavy mist. Within minutes, the inky skies opened, releasing torrential rains. Straining to see through the blur of reflected lights and passing motorists, she reduced her speed and concentrated. With the sound of an ambulance close behind, she pulled to the side of the road and watched it race by. Trying her best to relax, she switched on the radio. *The Little Drummer Boy* soothed her agitated mind. Turning down 17th Street, she searched for a parking spot near her favorite dining establishment. With umbrella in hand, and stomach rumbling, she followed the sidewalk leading to the Golden Dragon Restaurant. Before she reached her destination, the umbrella flipped inside out. Wiping away the rain from her flushed cheeks, she hurried inside. With greedy anticipation, she inhaled the tangy aroma of lemongrass and exotic spices. Tonight, was made for take-out. Yes, indeed.

The owner's teenage daughter, Liling, took her order before rushing back to the kitchen. In under a minute, the young woman returned with an enormous platter of sizzling beef and broccoli. After delivering the meal to a family of six, she absently pulled her ebony locks in a high ponytail and disappeared into the kitchen once again.

Jade took a seat on an emerald-green leather couch next to the register. Reclining against the backrest, she watched servers moving between tables with silver pots of hot tea. She recognized most of the waitresses were the owner's daughters. According to their mother, Quiyue Lee, the eldest was saving for her spring semester. Her mind drifted back to her academic career. College seemed like a lifetime ago. If she'd known then what she knew now, Jade probably would have taken classes relating to the occult. The information might help her understand some of the odd occurrences of the past few months. Trying not to dwell on the past, she turned her attention toward the window facing the hazy street.

A bright neon sign flashed intermittently, casting an electric blue hue through the sheets of rain and reflected headlights. As her mind wandered, the shrill cry of a siren broke through her web of daydreams. Glancing down at her cellphone, she realized fifteen minutes passed as she waited in hungry anticipation. The last time she'd visited the restaurant, Jade was accompanied by her best friends, Mary and Katie. They would be surprised to learn all the recent developments since they'd left Scotland. Without a doubt, she was eager to share her latest findings concerning Monarch Cove, especially the discovery of the Edwardian photograph and the bizarre ghostly encounters. But as much as she yearned to confide in her friends, she understood they were busy with their own lives. Katie was in the final planning phases of her upcoming Irish wedding, and Mary was torn between managing an art gallery and focusing on her new boyfriend, Deputy Rheinstein. Under the circumstances, it seemed unfair to place another mystery at their feet. No, this time she was determined to solve the puzzle on her own. And, of course, she had the undying support of her wonderful husband.

With the ring of a silver bell, Jade was presented with a cardboard box filled with three large plastic containers of sizzling hot and sour soup, steamed rice, and onion pancakes. With rain pelting her face, she headed back to her truck. Dougal crawled onto her lap as they drove home. When the truck's low beams illuminated the cottage, she released her pent-up breath. It took three trips to get the pets, dinner, and potted Christmas tree inside. After she'd locked the door and punched in the alarm code, she turned her attention to the fireplace.

The house was unusually chilly that evening and she shivered preparing the hearth. After moving the Douglas fir inside the living room, she breathed a sigh of relief, inhaling the tangy scent of pine. Decorating the tree would have to wait until after dinner. Even without ornaments, the fire-light casting its golden glow across the conifer branches made for a lovely show. Soon, the sound of crackling firewood blended with the rhythm of rain hitting the tin roof. Before preparing dinner for her and the pets, Jade lit the candelabra atop the mantel. Once aflame, she did the same for the matching set resting on the dining room table. With the intensity of the storm, it was just a matter of time, not if, they would lose electricity. After changing into flannel pajamas and fuzzy slippers, she filled Dougal and Morrigan's bowls before warming her own dinner in the microwave.

After dinner and dishes, Jade poured a glass of local chardonnay, and powered up the laptop before taking a seat by the fireplace. A cold wind rattled the chimney while she googled articles relating to 1906 Carmel,

Monarch Cove, and the mysterious disappearance of Lady Deidre O'Shea. For the next couple of hours, she pored through article after article of historical facts and unsettling urban legends. The disappearance of the young bride was never solved, notwithstanding numerous inquiries. Despite the lack of evidence, an abundance of theories concerning Deidre O'Shea's fate were soon uncovered. Most experts cried foul play, while some took on a more paranormal approach. Just as she was finishing an article called, "Ghostly Visitations of Monarch Cove," a howling downdraft roared from the chimney, sending tiny sparks into the air. When Jade stood from the couch to get a closer look, Dougal rushed to her side, a deep growl escaping his bristly muzzle. Staring toward the mantel, the terrier released a series of barks and howls.

"It's alright, boy," Jade said, glancing instinctively toward the portrait. By the glow of candlelight, the mysterious woman appeared to turn on her heel. As she studied the detailed oil painting, the power flickered before going out.

"There's a surprise," she whispered to herself. She reached for the candelabra and moved the flickering light toward the canvas. In the darkened room, the Edwardian lady appeared closer to the shore. Beneath the satin fringe of the gown, a dainty boot peaked beneath the lacy hemline.

"Not again," Jade whispered, gazing toward the phantom portrait.

Was it really changing? She stared at the tiny Edwardian shoe beneath the skirting of her dress. *Was the mysterious lady in grey heading toward the sea, or was this something entirely different? Could the alteration possibly be a hint of communication from the other side? Madame Garnier suggested a thin veil separated the living from the dead. And if that wasn't frightening enough, spirits could make their voices known. If this portrait did indeed belong to Deidre O'Shea, could she be reaching out by means of her art? If so, what did she want? How could she help her? What if a spirit meant her harm? If this was a portal, who else might be able to access it?* Each scenario multiplied her questions tenfold. How would she know for sure?

Jade pushed a lock of sandy-blonde hair behind her ear. Why is this happening when Aidan's at work? she thought, missing him terribly. If only he was home, holding her in his protective embrace. Together, they could figure it all out.

Several minutes passed as she studied the image, flickering candlelight playing against the slick canvas. The intensity of the storm battered the sides of the cottage, causing Dougal to whimper and tremble against his mistress's slippers.

Before Jade had time to walk back to the couch, she heard a buzzing sound resonating inside the living room. Placing her hands to her ears, she stumbled toward her dog, and gathered him in her arms. "Are we having an earthquake?" Jade cried, moving away from the fireplace. A blur of ivory wings blew by as Morrigan landed onto the back of the couch. The room shook and shuddered as the noise strengthened. She'd heard the sound before but couldn't quite place it. As she moved toward the couch, the portrait flew from its hanger, landing just inches from her trembling form.

"Oh, God!" Jade screamed, jumping backward. Dougal's high-pitched bark snapped her back to reality.

"Are you okay, boy?" she asked as the terrier leapt from her arms and rushed toward the fallen artwork. Once she consoled the frightened Scottie, she turned her attention back to the portrait. With trembling hands, she reached for the canvas, turning it upright from the floor. Although the room no longer quaked, and the terrible buzzing had stopped, she was over-whelmed with a sense of impending doom. Trying not to focus on anything besides her curiosity, she reached for the portrait. But when her hand grazed the back of the painting, she felt a raised area she hadn't noticed before. Turning the portrait upright, she studied a rectangular object behind the paper backing. Chewing her bottom lip, she moved her fingers around the raised edges.

Curious as to what it could be, she carried the portrait over to the dining room table, setting the canvas side down. After retrieving a pair of kitchen scissors, she held her breath, preparing herself for what could be behind the parchment. Lightning lit up the kitchen window, followed by a boom of thunder overhead. Carefully, and deftly, she cut into the paper, revealing the mystery waiting inside. She listened to the pouring rain, her body trembling in anticipation. A leather-bound diary was revealed in the flickering candlelight.

Chapter Nine

IT TOOK SEVERAL MOMENTS BEFORE JADE COULD PROCESS HER DISCOVERY. Dougal was not helping the situation, barking and circling the table with raised hackles.

"It's okay, boy," Jade said, kneeling to pet the anxious terrier. Before opening the diary, she decided to return the portrait to its original setting. After taking a closer look at the lady in grey, she fetched a ladder from the coat closet and propped it beneath the fireplace. After securing the canvas back in its place, she carried the diary to the living room and took a seat on the couch.

As she studied the leather front, her mind raced with questions.

Was this really happening? Could it be the diary of Deidre O'Shea? Why hadn't she noticed it the first time she hung the portrait? Did it become dislodged during the fall? Was the grey lady's fate recorded in the pages of the journal?

Jade knew from experience that entire lifetimes lived within the secret pages of diaries. After reading her great-grandmother's trek across the Oregon Trail, her life changed forever. And the same could be said for her husband discovering his great-grandmother's diaries. Edina MacFie revealed her secret selkie life inside a collection of leather-bound books.

Normally, Jade would have dived right in, but something told her this was not going to be a happy tale. After taking a sip of tangy chardonnay, she moved the candelabra to the edge of the coffee table for better lighting and opened the diary. The scent of jasmine wafted from the yellowed pages. While the wind and the rain battered the modest cottage, Jade lost herself to the pages of the past.

⚜

November 22nd, 1906
    Dear Diary,

It's been several weeks since my last passage. I've only recently emerged from an extraordinarily dark and painful episode of melancholia. Being locked away in the dank attic nearly robbed me of the will to live. My entire existence has been a hellish nightmare without means of escape. Oh, how I've yearned to flee from the oppressive walls of Monarch Cove, far away from the endless torments inflicted by my cruel husband. Little did I know whom I'd married until it was too late. I blame myself for giving in so easily to my aunt's demands. She insisted I would lead a rich and pros-perous life with Mr. O'Shea. With his considerable wealth and social stature, I was sure to be provided for. Lord knows my family struggled over the years. My poor parents both died so young, working themselves to the bone for a mere scrap. It would be a falsehood if I said his privilege was not desirable. On paper, he appeared to be the perfect gentleman. Yet, there was something off about my future husband. I just couldn't put my finger on it. Words fail me when I try to explain it.

Thomas O'Shea is twenty years my senior, an immigrant from Tipper-ary, Ireland. Strangely, Thomas attempts to hide his brogue, seemingly ashamed of his Celtic heritage. Although he offers a pleasant countenance and desirable physique, there's a remoteness in his eyes that turns my blood cold. In the beginning, he flattered me with his attention, showering me with gifts and promises during our short courtship. Sadly, he withheld his true nature until it was too late. If I'd only trusted my instincts. I should have known better. But here I am, a prisoner in this grand estate. Never have I known such terror.

The day he locked me away in the attic, a part of my soul died. I shudder even now, remembering the sound of the bolted door shutting behind me. It was a nightmare I couldn't escape. And the terrible darkness!

Only a thin beam of light pierced through a tiny opening in the board-covered window. If not for the small mercy, I think I would have gone entirely mad. The humiliations were endless, being kept from a bath or mirror, and a horrid chamber pot that was never cleaned. Lying upon a filthy mattress each night until I cried myself to sleep. Even weeks after the ordeal, my mind travels back to the horror. I wake up in the early morning hours, fearing I'm locked away again. Sometimes I sit on the back porch, gazing toward the sea. If only I could find myself floating along with the current, perhaps my soul could drift away with the churning tides.

Yet, when I stood on the edge of the abyss, all hope extinguished, a beacon of light shone through the halls of Monarch Cove. Do I dare even write these words? My dear Johnathon. My savior. When I gazed into his beautiful brown eyes, I realized God, in his infinite mercy, sent me an angel. If only we'd met before I took my vows. Oh, how life would be so different! But fate dealt me a vicious hand with Mr. O'Shea. And then, when all seemed lost, a beautiful soul saved me. In a few short weeks, I will cast away the chains of bondage and escape with Johnathon. I count the moments until Christmas Eve. My love and I will sail to the Emerald Isle, to freedom and our new lives in lovely Tipperary.

December 23rd, 1906

It is with great risk and peril I write these words. If my writings were ever discovered, all hope would be lost. To prevent this from happening, I've sewed an extra lining beneath my petticoats to keep you, dear diary, away from the wandering eyes of my husband. At night, I place my precious journal behind the binding of my canvas. Although I do this at great risk, I must write my thoughts down to keep my wits. How do I even put to words my great love? Oh, of course he's handsome and strong, and has the most beautiful whiskey-colored eyes. His charming Irish brogue sets my heart aflame...all these things. But it's his kindness and gentle nature that makes my soul soar. If only we could have met before being betrothed to my wicked husband. How my life would be different. I could move freely, unencumbered by shame and Thomas's never-ending cruelties. Even the chance to live in a modest hut with my lover to the end of days, I'd gladly trade all the trappings of Monarch Cove. Ha! I wouldn't even mind sharing Johnathon's cabin by the sea. A modest abode, but oh, the passion I've felt between those beloved walls. Never have I been more alive. And yes, I know I've sinned. But I pray God will forgive me in his great compassion. For I have married a monster. I hope and pray we can be successful in our escape attempt. But I fear we will never be free if we stay in the States. So, we will journey to Tipperary, Ireland and live a modest life. Perhaps I will find work as a seamstress once again. And my lover will fish upon the glorious seas. We will pursue our art when time permits. For now, I will count the hours until freedom.

One more day.

Dear Diary,

I have no idea to the date or time of my journal. My dream has turned into a nightmare. Oh, God, where do I begin? I've been in and out of consciousness for some time, apparently with fever. My ragged gown clings to my damp skin. I guess I should be grateful for the small kindness of finding my diary after the accident. When I awoke, I searched for a way to escape my prison. But horrors of horrors, I cannot find any way out. My greatest fears have come to fruition. And that is not all; oh no. I can no longer speak. My voice is gone. For my husband stole everything from me. My lover was not at the seashore as promised. When I arrived home Christmas morning, Thomas was waiting. After I gazed into his cruel eyes, I realized his guilt.

Manically laughing and cursing, he chased me through the manor, accusing me of adultery, addressing me as a little whore and other unspeakable names. When I told him that his nephew was more of a man than he could ever aspire to be, he slapped me across the mouth. It was not the first time he'd assaulted me physically. His satisfied eyes sent me into an oblivion of madness. He asked me how it was possible that a dead man could be a superior lover. My blood turned cold, realizing he'd confessed to murder. I do not know the details of his cruel act, but I had no doubt what he'd done. Enraged, I threw myself at his towering body, scratching and clawing his mocking face. There was murder in his eyes, so I ran toward the spiraling staircase with my husband in close pursuit. I'd nearly made it to the top when I felt his hands tighten around my throat, pressing with acute precision until the world turned grey.

When I awoke, I was lying atop a filthy mattress in the attic. Everything appears to mirror my imprisonment last summer. When I open my mouth to scream, nothing escapes but a raspy cough. And then I feel the pain. Hot and alive, a thousand knives piercing my crushed vocal cords. I've tried to block the truth from my mind, fearing my abysmal fate. Yet the terrible reality remains. I'm a mute. Is the affliction permanent? What has Thomas done to me? Time is ephemeral and I wonder if I ever really left the attic to begin with. Did I imagine it all? No, I know Johnathon was real. Vaguely, my husband's words come to mind. Was he speaking the truth when he told me Johnathon was dead? Could there be any chance my lover survived? Perhaps he's a prisoner as well? Surely it might be possible. How could Thomas kill his only nephew? The truth whispers, but I shy away from it. I must hold onto the memory of Johnathon's beautiful face. Perhaps there's a way out of my prison. For some inexplicable reason, a kerosene lamp was left behind. There's still a bit of oil remaining and a few matches. I must be careful to use it sparingly. Drifting in and out of consciousness, days and nights flow together. Other than a thread of morning light escaping through the boarded window, there is nothing but endless darkness. Sadly, it disappears soon after dawn rises in the east. Sometimes I hear vague footsteps down the hall. When I pound on the walls, it is of no avail. The once smooth wallpapered walls of my art studio are now boarded over with impregnable planks of wood. Scratching and scraping the endless barrier suggests I'm forever sealed within one enormous coffin. The thought is beyond terrifying. I've become a ghost residing in the walls of Monarch Cove. After I awoke a short while ago, I turned on my lamp. It's unbearably cold today. For some reason, my seascape painting remains on an easel in the back of the room. It's a small mercy, for I was able to find my diary, pen, and ink beneath the back. The rest of my art supplies and comforts have been removed.

I don't know how many days have passed since I last took to pen. When will he let me out? Surely this punishment will end soon. Does he know I'm aware of his murderous ways? What will be my fate?

Dear Diary,

My hand aches as I write this passage. Something terrible occurred which I'm not sure I can even put into words. Every strike of the pen set my fingers aflame with white hot agony. Where do I even begin? I stare at the portrait now for days and nights on end. In complete darkness, I conjure every detail of my beloved canvas. Time runs together. With nothing else to do, I pace the walls of my tomblike abode, trying to keep my blood flowing. I fear if I lay idle too long, I may not have the strength to wake up. Not that it would be the worst possible outcome. Although, there is a small desire to live. Sadly, it diminishes with each passing second. The isolation is terrible. I'm torn from waiting for the door to open and fearing it will.

Thomas arrives once a day, usually late in the evening, and shoves a tray of food and water across the floor, quickly locking the door behind him. My husband leaves without a word. I believe he waits until the servants are asleep before setting the meal inside. He provides only table scraps, and I must be careful to make them last until his next visit. Last evening the unthinkable happened. My usual supper, though often meager and stale, was not delivered. I waited for hours, pounding away at my prison walls to no avail. It's useless to try to scream since the accident. After what seemed like an eternity, Mr. O'Shea burst into the room enraged and reeking of bourbon. After tossing a loaf of bread to the floor, he watched me crawl like an animal to the pathetic meal, ripping into it with relish. All the while, Thomas smirked while I groveled, a small smile on his ruddy face.

When I'd finished, he stood over me with lantern in hand. I dared not move, fearing what he might be capable of. With a slurring voice, he announced that he was remarrying, and I must stay quiet, or he would take away more than just my freedom. As tears streaked down my face, he kneeled beside me. Taking me into his arms, he stroked my matted hair. At first, he appeared to be showing mercy, but when his hands began to explore elsewhere, I realized his sinful intentions. How I fought with the last ounce of my strength, raking him across the face, even leaving bloody trails with my fingernails! He screamed in rage and grabbed my right hand, squeezing until the bones splintered beneath his grip. Unimaginable pain exploded as I curled upon the floor clutching my mangled fingers to my bosom. His laughter echoed down the hallway, shouting how I would never paint again. Once alone, I realized Thomas left his lantern behind. In the soft glow, I gazed toward my painting, my only salvation in a hellish existence. I could not survive without my last glimpse of the outside world.

I must have slipped into unconsciousness soon after, for I committed a fateful mistake. I left the kerosene burning. By morning, both lamps were empty. While the final stretch of light fades from the tiny partition of driftwood, I attempt to memorize the portrait one final time before darkness descends. If I stare long enough, the frothy waves appear to glisten beneath the dying light of dawn. I breathe the balmy aroma of the sea and listen to the waves crash along the shore. Sometimes I can see my lover's cabin in the distance. Seagulls cry as they fly over the tin roof. Did the door move slightly? Yes, I believe it did. Surely it will open soon. Perhaps Johnathon is behind the oak barrier, waiting to take me away. Beloved, please find me now.

Dear Diary,

I am hopelessly indisposed. Without food, water, and sunlight, I fear my time on this earthly plane is short. As far as I loathe my cruel husband, realizing he's gone seals my dismal fate. Voices of the past echo throughout Monarch Cove, allowing glimpses of the present. Mr. O'Shea is remarrying. This leaves me in a terrible predicament. Did my husband truly abandon me to my cold tomb? Although my hunger is intense, it's the unbearable thirst which brings me to my knees in anguish. Only a spark of life left, longing for release from the agony of living. When I woke a short while ago, I noticed my canvas glowing and pulsing in the darkness. I'm at a loss to understand how it's possible, but I'm grateful for the occurrence. A gleaming essence surrounds the easel, revealing my beloved seaside cove. If I stare long enough, the cabin door in the distance appears to open. Particles of light dance along the edges of darkness, illuminating the canvas to my delight. Long shadows spread across the white sands as another long day comes to an end. Past and present overlap and I'm not certain what is real anymore.

Where is my beloved Johnathon? The torture of not knowing is driving me mad. My only reprieve from my anguish is gazing at my beloved portrait.

Although I no longer paint, fingers crushed beyond repair, my final artwork remains on the easel. Why my husband left it behind in the attic is still a mystery. Perhaps it's simply a reminder of what was stolen from me. The seashore was my only escape from the foreboding walls of Monarch Cove. I remember every tender moment with my beloved. Thomas will never take away my memories! When I close my eyes, I feel my beloved's caress, listening to the sound of the sea's evocative mysteries. What I wouldn't give to experience one more moment in Johnathon's protective arms. Oh, how my lover opened my eyes to endless enchantments. I will always be grateful for our short time together. If I never leave this room, I can make peace with knowing true love does exist.

My soul blossomed one summer afternoon beneath garnet skies. God, give me the will to hold onto the memories and take them with me when I leave. So, now, I consider my canvas, lost in the shadows of yesterday. When my hunger is overwhelming, the delicious aroma of abalone stew teases my senses. And when my merciless prison becomes unbearable, and an icy chill moves me toward the brink of madness, a pinpoint of light flickers on the horizon. Sometimes, the ocean glistens, and I dare say the intoxicating scent of jasmine lingers. And I gaze toward Johnathon's cabin overlooking the rocky cliffside. Tonight, the door is ajar. If I can just find the strength to crawl across the damp floor, toward the cliffside. Oh, God, I must find him before the light fades forever. Please wait for me, my love...

※

JADE TURNED THE PAGE AND FOUND IT BLANK. SHE SHOOK HER HEAD, trembling from the horrid tale. No more passages. Did Mr. O'Shea really leave his wife alone to die in the damp attic? Could he be so cruel to enjoy his honeymoon, sentencing Deidre to a slow, painful death? Did she finally find peace at the end? Was it possible Johnathon found her by means of the portrait? Or was she trapped between worlds like Madame Garnier suggested?

The buzzing of her cell phone snapped her back to reality. Seeing Aidan's name soothed her weary mind.

"Hello?" she whispered.

"What's wrong? Ye sound spooked."

"It's been a strange night."

"Did you lose power?" Aidan asked.

"We did. And the portrait fell off the mantel shortly afterward."

"Oh, no. Are you okay?"

"Yes, but you'll never believe what I found," Jade said.

"What, darlin'?"

"Deidre O'Shea's diary."

There was silence on the other side of the phone.

"Aidan?"

"Sorry, I'm still here. Just can't believe this is happening. I don't want you to be alone right now."

"Well, I'll be fine. Don't worry about me."

"I always worry about you, lass. God, this is troubling," Aidan said.

"I know, but there's nothing either one of us can do just yet. I'm going to bed in a few minutes. I'll be fine."

"Are you sure?"

"Yes, I'm sure. I appreciate you so much. Can't wait for you to come back home," Jade said.

"Aye, looking forward to holding you in my arms again. Please call if anything else happens, alright?"

"I will. Love you."

"Love you, too. Hope you get a good night's sleep," Aidan said.

After Jade clicked off her phone, she readied herself for bed. She carried the candelabra to the bathroom and washed her face and brushed her teeth. After blowing out the candles, she slipped into bed with Dougal snuggling close. As for pleasant dreams, they were few. She tossed and turned dreaming of Deidre O'Shea locked away in the attic.

Chapter Ten

THE NEXT COUPLE OF WEEKS BLENDED WITHOUT A HINT OF PARANORMAL activity. Jade focused on preparations for the antique shop's Christmas Eve party. Aidan's schedule prevented him from attending, but he promised to make up his absence after work. She looked forward to spending the holidays together. If all went as planned, they would enjoy four uninterrupted days together.

The afternoon of the party, Jade finished organizing holiday decorations, along with preparing a bountiful spread of appetizers and Champagne for her guests. Unlike the previous grand opening, she found herself handling the entire event by herself. Katie and Mary were busy with their own growing businesses, and she didn't want to burden them during the holidays. She looked forward to catching up after things settled down. Although she expected her friends' absence, she was surprised Madame Garnier failed to show up for the party. The psychic RSVP'd early in the week and even offered to help at the register. When Jade called the psychic's cellphone, it went directly to voicemail. After placing the phone back in her purse, she noticed one of her regular customers making her way to the front of the line. Millie Blackwell placed a ruby-colored glass bell onto the wooden counter. They made small talk as Jade wrapped Millie's latest purchase. The vivacious grandmother visited the antique shop weekly, always searching for the perfect heirloom to add to her growing collection.

Jade suspected that she was on a fixed income, as she often paid for her antiques from a tattered change purse, which appeared decades old. With lips pursed, Mrs. Blackwell carefully counted her coins, lining them neatly by the register. Jade made certain to offer her devoted customer the senior discount, often selling at cost.

Snapping her purse closed, Millie gushed over her latest acquisition, a Fenton ruby petite bell adorned with white roses. Jade smiled as the grand-mother gathered up her package, promising to visit again soon. Despite the festive atmosphere and lively foot traffic, an unsettling feeling dampened her mood. Trying her best to ignore the rising anxiety, she focused on her customers, making small talk and ringing up sales.

By the end of the evening, Jade was feeling both fatigued and light-headed. She hoped she wasn't getting a cold or flu, considering she would be sharing the first Christmas with her husband. And an even more trou-bling thought shadowed her mind, but she pushed it away, admonishing herself for letting her imagination get the best of her. Trying to put on a brave face despite feeling under the weather, she mingled with her customers and offered them appetizers and flutes of Champagne.

With over three hours of favorable sales, and compliments on her shop, Jade called it a night. After packing up the pets, she made her way down Lighthouse Ave. Before heading home, she searched for a parking place in front of the local pharmacy. Thrumming her fingers on the steering wheel, she tried to summon her courage. Chewing on her lower lip, a dozen thoughts flashed through her mind.

"You're just being silly, but better to be safe than sorry," she whispered to herself. Dougal cocked his head to the side, watching his owner place a trembling hand on the driver-side door. Once inside CVS, Jade hurried down an empty aisle, heart thrumming and cheeks flushed. What she was imagining couldn't possibly be a reality. She was probably being paranoid. After all, she was only a week late, and was certain it was due to all the excitement during the past month. Even so, she thought it best to air on the side of caution. Studying several boxes of pregnancy tests, she reached for one advertising early detection and quick results. It's only been a few weeks since our honeymoon. What are the odds? she thought. Of course, we haven't been exactly practicing birth control, have we? Nope. We'd waited so long to be intimate; it was the last thing on both of our minds. Jade tried distracting herself on the ride back home, focusing on a romantic evening with her husband, but the nagging feeling just wouldn't let up. *It will be negative*, she told herself. After the test, I'll tell Aidan and we'll have a good laugh about it. Yes, that's how it will go. At least she hoped...

MADAME GARNIER MOVED TOWARD THE DINING ROOM TABLE IN A FOG. HER tea had long grown cold. As her dark eyes rolled backward in their sockets, troubling visions flooded her mind. The lady in grey was emerging through the veil. Unfortunately, she was not alone. The Dark One followed closely behind. Tonight, he would make his way into the realm of the living. The fight between good and evil would hang in the balance. The psychic-medium called upon her ancestors, praying for their support. Soon, they would battle for a soul caught between worlds. Pyewacket the Cat purred; his emerald eyes fixed on his mistress. The wind whipped the sides of the bungalow, and the candles flickered in the frigid room.

Chapter Eleven

Jade was relieved when she returned home after the Christmas Eve party. Anticipating Aidan's return from work any minute, she prepared for his arrival. The presents were wrapped, and stockings hung. She wanted everything to be perfect for her new husband. While hail peppered the tin roof, she set holiday scented candles around her clawfoot tub. Three days away from her lover made her yearn for his powerful embrace.

Carefully, she removed the pregnancy test from the paper bag and read the directions. Too nervous to find out the result just yet, she placed the box inside the cupboard below the sink. "Maybe after my bath," she whispered. Feeling better about her decision, she undressed in the soft glow, shivering as cool air crept beneath the bathroom door. While the clawfoot tub filled with rose-scented bubbles, Jade set a tissue-lined box with sage-green lingerie onto the cherrywood countertop. Tonight, she planned to surprise her lover with silk and lace. She lifted her shapely legs into the tub and eased herself into the warm water, enjoying the flickering candlelight while listening to the distant sound of pounding surf.

Jade reached for her novel next to the bath. Sinking further down into the warm water, she pulled a small table across the tub which she used for reading, and on romantic evenings, a glass of her favorite wine. But tonight, chardonnay was replaced by a mug of herbal tea. She grimaced as her stomach clenched. Probably just a stupid stomach bug, she thought to herself. She sipped the hot tea and leaned back, eagerly anticipating another thrilling chapter from Emily Brontë's Wuthering Heights. It was one of her favorite classics, perfect for a stormy evening. Within moments, she was lost within the pages of the gothic tale.

'The intense horror of nightmare came over me: I tried to draw back my arm, but the hand clung to it, and a most melancholy voice sobbed, 'Let me in - let me in!' 'Who are you?' I asked, struggling, meanwhile, to disengage myself. 'Catherine Linton,' it replied, shiveringly (why did I think of LINTON? I had read EARNSHAW twenty times for Linton) - 'I'm come home: I'd lost my way on the moor!' As it spoke, I discerned, obscurely, a child's face looking through the window.'

As the scene unfolded, thunder boomed overhead, and gale winds shook the cottage walls.

A sharp growl sounding from the living room snapped her back to reality. A high-pitched howl followed. Jade sighed, imagining Dougal was anxious concerning the evening's storm. She placed her bookmark inside the beloved novel and moved the reading table to the side of the tub.

Reluctantly, she left the warmth of her bath, and hastily dried off with an oversized towel. Before checking on the terrier, she slipped into the silky lingerie and covered herself in a satin robe and matching slippers. With her damp curls wrapped in a towel, she wandered into the living room.

"What's the matter, boy? Are you afraid of the storm, buddy?" The smile on her face faltered when she noticed Dougal's raised hackles. An icy chill prickled her spine as she watched her dog cowering in the corner of the room.

"Who's there?" Jade whispered, trying to make sense of her surroundings. The firelight flickered as she listened to the terrier's low growl. "It's all right, Dougal," she said, trying her best to keep her voice steady. A shrill buzzing sounded near the couch. The odd noise was followed by a heavy mist swirling above the beige cushions. As the specter pulled energy from the room, Jade was unable to look away. Within seconds, the hazy form of a middle-aged gentleman solidified. Wearing a dark three-piece suit, he sipped from a glass filled with an amber-colored beverage. Condensation reflected the glow of the firelight. A cawing from the bedroom sounded before Morrigan swept across the living room toward the intruder. Moments before her razor-sharp talons grazed the apparition's opaque flesh, the raven was struck down to the ground with a wave of his large hand.

"Morrigan!" Jade shouted, moving toward her pet. The bird ruffled its feathers before flying toward Jade's raised arm. Once balanced, she edged closer to her mistress, nudging Jade's ashen cheek with the back of her pale beak. Relieved, she reached for the ivory raven with a trembling hand.

"Lass, the next time your creature approaches, I will not be so generous. Tell me where Deidre is hiding and perhaps, I'll spare you. If not, your home will be covered by your pets' blood and bones. And, I dare say, you will join them soon after," the ghostly visitor replied.

He chuckled before taking a sip of whiskey, his muddy eyes never leaving Jade's grey ones. She took a slow breath, trying not to panic. The man appeared as spirit, but his reality was abundantly clear. To her amazement, she noticed tiny drops of precipitation rising from his glass.

"I don't know what you're talking about. Who is Deidre?" she asked, backing away from the apparition, guessing, yet unbelieving as to whom he was. Deidre's husband.

"Don't play games with me, lass! Her portrait rests above your mantel," he said, gesturing toward the fireplace. Jade shuddered, noticing his razor-sharp fingernails.

The spirit—Thomas—leaned forward in his seat, licking his bottom lip in agitation.

"The seascape is her doorway to the other side. She's been here. I can smell the cloying aroma of her jasmine perfume. I'll ask one more time. If you value your life, think carefully before you answer."

Reflective firelight mirrored his blood-shot eyes while he scanned Jade's hour-glass figure, eyeing the curves beneath her lacy robe. "Then again, perhaps we can have a bit of fun while we wait," he said. "You look young and vital. Yes, I think I'd enjoy a taste," Thomas said, his dark gaze boring into her.

With that, the phantom rose from the couch, placing his drink upon the table. When he smiled, Jade gasped. For his teeth were needle-sharp, and an eerie grin stretched impossibly wide, moving towards his earlobes. Jade screamed while Dougal howled, and a high-pitched shriek sounded by the fireplace.

A translucent form pixilated in front of the hearth, miniscule bursts of light shimmering through the darkness. In terror, Jade glanced up at the phantom portrait. The Edwardian figure vanished, now only an empty seashore remained. When the apparition solidified, Deidre O'Shea stood protectively in front of Jade's trembling body.

"Do not be afraid. He is not here for you." As the grey lady took her hand, Jade released her breath. Despite the chill of her ghostly flesh, the sensation was surprisingly comforting.

The male specter clapped his menacing hands together, and the sound echoed in the fire-lit room.

"Oh, my darling bride. You can speak! Ha! But I did so enjoy you more when you couldn't."

The corners of his mouth lifted as he moved from the shadows. "You took so long to come to me. I was getting ready to enjoy this fine lass. But now that you're here, we will have a proper party! You've been running all these years, but you couldn't run forever. Submit yourself body and soul, Lady O'Shea, for you belong to me. Don't imagine death will separate us now. Acquiesce or I'll destroy everything in this room," Thomas said, reaching his talon-like hands toward his first wife.

Jade recoiled, realizing his nails resembled claws. Before she realized what was happening, Deidre's fingers splayed out, shooting diamonds of light across the room. The particles surrounded Dougal, Morrigan, and Jade in a soothing amber halo.

"What are you doing?" Jade asked, gazing into Deidre's hazel eyes.

"Thomas will not harm your pets, but we must leave at once before my power weakens. Listen to your gift and follow me," Lady O'Shea whispered. As Jade nodded, the spirit took her hands. Together, they experienced gravity releasing its hold. Jade trembled as the mysterious woman gazed into her eyes. "To the portrait." Glancing in confusion, her instincts told her to obey. "Never take your eyes off the waves!" Deidre O'Shea shouted.

"No!" Thomas O'Shea yelled, lunging forward. The women watched in horror as the male apparition's eyes turned citrine yellow. Simultaneously, the women propelled toward the phantom portrait with Morrigan close behind. When they reached the canvas, Jade felt a tingly sensation sweep through her body before speeding through a kaleidoscope of light and sound. In astonishment, she found herself on the shadowy side of the veil.

Chapter Twelve

GLANCING AT THE DOG CARRIER ON THE FRONT PASSENGER SEAT, AIDAN drove home with a wide grin. As he reached for the seatbelt holding it in place, a tiny white puppy licked his hand through the mesh covering. A bright emerald bow was fastened to the top of the petite kennel. He hoped Jade would enjoy her Christmas present. His wife mentioned several times owning a toy poodle when she was a little girl. He remembered the way her beautiful grey eyes sparkled when she spoke of her beloved childhood dog. As luck had it, Madame Garnier reached out in early December, suggesting Aidan consider adopting a dog at the local SPCA. Believing a new addition to the family would be a perfect Christmas present for his new bride, the fireman visited the shelter during his lunch break. The psychic-medium introduced him to the staff, and he soon realized he was being offered the pick of the litter. Amused, he noticed the basket of squirming puppies wiggling about their collection of donated blankets. A velvet-soft muzzle peaked through the pile, and the runt wiggled her way toward Aidan. Grinning, he admired her dark button eyes and white fluffy coat. The petite pup was curious and friendly, licking his face frantically as he stroked her behind the ears. When he held her in his arms, he knew she'd be a perfect addition to the family. The staff explained that both the puppy's vaccinations and spay surgery would be finished in two weeks, perfect time for the holidays. On Christmas Eve, Aidan officially adopted their new family member and headed home, excited to spend the holidays with his beautiful wife and their beloved pets.

After parking on the cobblestone driveway, he balanced the dog carrier and box of supplies before heading inside the cottage. Aidan's contentment quickly vanished when he heard Dougal's frantic howls from the living room. Gently setting down the kennel, he rushed toward the frightened terrier whimpering beneath the phantom portrait. The firefighter's mouth fell open in disbelief. Within the middle of the canvas, two figures faced the viewer. To his astonishment, he realized the grey lady was no longer alone. A painted version of his wife stood by her side while Morrigan the Raven flew across the ebbing tides. Trying to remain calm, his eyes darted across the living room. The tangy scent of bourbon hung in the air. Moving toward the end table by the couch, he noted the abandoned whiskey glass. When he bent down to take a closer look, he spotted a damp bath towel discarded nearby. With his heart jack hammering against his ribcage, Aidan lifted the terrycloth to his nose, breathing in the aroma of rose-scented bubble bath. Teeth clenched and hands curled into fists, Laird MacFie darted toward the bedroom calling his wife's name, with Dougal in quick pursuit.

MADAME GARNIER WAS SERVING HER BELOVED CATS THEIR SUPPER WHEN the visions began. Dropping a can of Fancy Feast to the linoleum floor, she stumbled toward the dining room table, sinking heavily into a velvet-backed chair. Pyewacket the Cat jumped onto the psychic's lap to soothe his beloved mistress. While her favorite feline purred and kneaded, a flood of images flashed simultaneously in her mind's eye. The mysterious Grey Lady was pursued by a dark presence. The MacFie's cottage appeared, overlapping a misty image of the phantom portrait. Two lost souls joined Jade Mackenzie, intersecting the ephemeral veils between the living and the dead. When the shadows passed, she stroked the back of Pyewacket's ebony head and released a pent-up breath. Gazing down at her familiar, she whispered, "Tonight's journey will be full of phantoms and shadows. Stay close in spirit, sweet boy." Madame Garnier gathered her keys and purse and headed into the storm.

Chapter Thirteen

AN EXPLOSION OF LIGHT AND SOUND FLOODED JADE'S SENSES AS SHE WAS pulled through a vast tunnel. Music sounded from afar, but she couldn't place the melody. What she understood as reality simultaneously transformed into a blended consciousness of divine understanding. Memories of her childhood flashed before her steel-grey eyes, like a movie projector from long ago. Glimpses of family members flickered in the distance, just out of reach. The song of her ancestors floated on the wind. With sublime gratitude, she noted their presence, realizing they'd stood by her side every step of the way. A feeling of peace radiated from her heart and soul, and all anxiety melted away. "I must remember this moment," she whispered to herself. "Love is all around us. One is never truly alone. We belong to the Eternal." As her heart swelled with the realization, a familiar voice made her heart ache with longing.

"You're safe, darling girl. Have no fear." She listened to her grandmother's soothing encouragement. From the ephemeral veil, a second spirit manifested. Jade held her breath as her mother's form solidified. A spectrum of vivid colors haloed the familiar silhouette.

She watched in awe as the shimmering pair held hands and smiled.

"Look at my lovely daughter. I'm so proud of her, Mother. My baby's grown into a beautiful young woman."

Tears-streaked Jade's face as she felt her mother's hands press down onto her shoulders and soft lips grazed her forehead. Closing her eyes, she inhaled the familiar aroma of rose petals and clean linen.

How long she remained in the void, she wasn't certain. Time presented differently on the other side. Eventually, she found herself alone, standing at the edge of a rocky cliff overlooking a raging sea. Muted ocean waves cascaded over a charcoal-grey shore. Hearing foot-steps behind, she turned to watch Deidre O'Shea approaching with kerosene lamp in hand. Absently, the specter pushed a lock of dark curls from her pale face.

"Jade MacFie, stay close by my side. Now that the Dark One noticed you, he will pursue your soul until the bitter end. Thomas O'Shea tormented my soul for decades. This time, he intends to destroy me at all costs," Deidre said, reaching for Jade's hand.

Before she took it, she turned to watch Morrigan the Raven flying across the inky sky, ribbons of moonlight dancing across her pearly feathers.

"Morrigan?" Jade called.

"Your raven crossed the veil, being she is your familiar."

"But where is Dougal?" Jade asked, fearing for her dog's safety.

"Your terrier remains at the cottage. Before we parted, I released a protective halo around his aura. Nothing will harm him. However, we are both in grave danger as my husband will arrive shortly. There is no time to lose. Please stay close. We must hurry," Deidre said, reaching out her ghostly fingers.

Feeling overwhelmed, Jade grasped Lady O'Shea's hand, wincing at the coldness of her flesh. Together, they rushed toward the abandoned cabin overlooking the churning tides. Deidre raised her kerosene lamp, illumi-nating the empty shack.

"Where are we?" Jade asked.

"My past, my home, a prison of memories. This modest cabin once belonged to my beloved. We were supposed to meet long ago to start our lives anew, but my husband put a stop to it. He's the wickedest of men, torturing me in both life and death."

"Are you Deidre O'Shea?"

The dark-haired woman locked eyes with Jade. "I am. Or I was. Past and present no longer hold meaning for me. My only wish is for my love to return. I must find Johnathon before it's too late. Please, I beg you to help me. I know you have the gift of sight and might assist me in my hour of need. You're my only hope."

"I have so many questions, Mrs. O'Shea."

"Please, call me Deidre. My friends always did. Until I became a fine lady of course. But the luxury came with a terrible price. For you see, I married a monster. An evil man whose presence haunts me even now."

Jade's eyes glistened with tears as she regarded the apparition.

"Yes, I heard your tragic story. I discovered your journal when the portrait fell from my fireplace. I apologize, but I was desperate to find answers, so I read your diary. I'm so sorry for what you endured," Jade said.

Deidre pushed a lock of brunette curls away from her ashen cheek. A small smile moved over her face.

"There is no need to apologize. I made certain you had access to my diary. I used the storm's energy to manifest that evening. It allowed me to send you a message from the other side. The portrait has been my way of reaching out between past and present. If you've ever wondered, your energy shines brightly through the veil."

Jade nodded. "I'm not entirely sure what's happening right now, but I'll help in any way I can. Just tell what you need."

Deidre steepled her hands together beneath her dimpled chin. "That's very kind. I'll try to explain what I know, but there are mysteries that still elude me. I don't fully understand my circumstances myself, but I can explain a few things. For over a century, I've wandered in a state of limbo. The portrait hanging above your fireplace, my final artwork, was the last image I gazed upon before leaving the world of the living. As you know from reading my diary, my husband abandoned me in the attic, sealed my fate, and in doing so, trapped my soul."

"I don't quite understand," Jade said.

Deidre's lips pinched together as she considered the abandoned cottage.

"Many years ago, Thomas O'Shea left me alone to die an agonizing death. After my passing, I awoke to a beautiful tunnel of light. My suffering ended, and an eternity of peace and tranquility beckoned me home. Joyfully, I moved toward the heavenly radiance, feeling the sublime love of God. Yet, when I stood on the threshold of the Divine, my heart filled with doubt. Had Johnathon crossed over to the light, or was he waiting for me within the walls of Monarch Cove? If so, would I miss my chance to be with him for eternity? The thought of losing my beloved a second time was unbearable. Trembling and uncertain, I turned away from the sublime." Deidre's jaw clenched as she recalled the memory. "Well, I would soon regret my decision." Mrs. O'Shea shuddered, crossing her arms over her chest. "Within moments, I found myself lost within a shadowy afterlife. Alone and desperate, I wandered the empty halls of Monarch Cove. To my surprise, doors no longer imprisoned me. So, I moved through the barriers with ease, clinging to the hope that Johnathon was somewhere nearby. This new world no longer held any trace of warmth or color, only shadows of the past. Time moves slowly within the veil; my agonizing search proved fruitless. Losing hope, and out of options, I eventually returned to Johnathon's cabin. The heavenly light vanished, and only the abandoned cabin remained. Slipping down onto the floor, I wept. Apparently, I'd given away my chance at paradise for nothing in return." Deidre's hazel eyes filled with tears. "In the end, I sealed my fate. Now, I'm cursed to roam the lonely grounds of Monarch Cove. I've asked myself many times if it was worth the sacrifice. Well, my answer may surprise you." Deidre walked across the abandoned cabin with a faraway look, her footsteps making no sound.

Fresh tears welled in her hazel eyes. "Yes, it was worth the pain and suffering. If only for the chance to find my one true love. Although it appears my future is grim, I pray Johnathon eventually found his way out of the darkness. If I could return to the eternal light, perhaps I would be gifted a second chance. As the years rolled by, I've wandered between planes of existence, endless corridors filled with shadow and sorrow. When my husband was among the living, I'd watch him going about his life, seemingly without a care in the world. He appeared unaffected by his sinful deeds. But that would eventually change, I made sure of it. When his second wife died, he slowly lost touch with reality. Instead of feeling pity for Thomas, my rage for him grew.

"One stormy night, I discovered I could appear to him. Oh, the revelation was delicious! From that time forward, I pursued him, waiting for the moments when he was full of drink and wrapped in a cloak of self-pity. Yes, the satisfaction of feeling his anguish was its own reward. Without a doubt, I relentlessly sought my revenge. Sadly, this enjoyment was stolen from me. One fateful evening, in a drunken fever, he screamed at my portrait in such manic rage his heart gave out. At first, I delighted in the knowledge the despicable man was dead. But to my horror, I discovered the terrible truth. His spirit refused to leave Monarch Cove." Deidre stepped closer to Jade.

"Since that night, Thomas O'Shea made it his mission to destroy me. There were many times he nearly succeeded, but I always found ways to elude him by means of my portrait. If I concentrated, I could use the painting as a portal. Once my spirit entered the canvas, I hid within the protection of the stormy seashore. My husband was unable to follow. After you took procession of my final artwork, I was able to escape Monarch Cove for longer periods of time. But I could only manifest briefly before I was pulled back through the veil. Interestingly, you were not the first person I reached out to. Over the years, the estate changed ownership. Whenever a new occupant took residence, I tried to make my presence known. My attempts proved fruitless until the most recent owner of Monarch Cove. Eventually, she became aware of my existence, but she was unable to assist me. In fact, I believe you met her just the other day," Deidre said.

Jade's brow raised, beginning to understand. "The real estate agent?" she asked.

"Yes, Mrs. Dunsmuir adored Monarch Cove. Near the end of her life, I was able to make contact. You see, souls sometimes become aware of deceased spirits shortly before their passing. Once Abby was cognizant of my presence, she became obsessed with me.

"At the time, the elderly lady suffered from advanced dementia. In her altered state, I was able to communicate. Sadly, she couldn't assist me other than listening to my story. After her death, Mrs. Dunsmuir refused to leave the manor. We occasionally cross paths, but she doesn't realize she's passed from the world of the living." Deidre shook her head. "But that's a story for another day. Time is short, so I will tell you what I remember after my accident. I believe the details I'm about to share may be beneficial in our quest tonight."

"Yes, please. I have so many questions," Jade said.

Deidre nodded and stepped closer. "This all must seem quite puzzling." Mrs. O'Shea ran her pale fingers over the doorframe, releasing a flurry of dust particles within the glow of the kerosene lantern.

"Once Thomas discovered my infidelity, he became enraged and maliciously planned his revenge. The evening of Johnathon's disappearance, I felt nothing but hatred for my husband. There was never a doubt in my mind he'd done something vile to his nephew. Our love was timeless, and I was certain Johnathon would never abandon me. During the Christmas Eve party, I left the manor to find him. After discovering his cabin empty, I searched along the shoreline, and down by the cliffs. For hours, I combed every inch of the cove. Exhausted and heartbroken, I reluctantly returned to Monarch Cove. In the soft rays of dawn, I noticed my husband waiting for me in the dining room. The servants had been given the day off, which was unusual. Thomas was tight with a penny and kept the staff working through the holidays even when I protested. There he sat, a small smile playing on his face, dressed in the same suit from the night before. When I gazed into his dark eyes, my blood ran cold. Deep down I knew something terrible happened to Johnathon. Without a doubt, my husband was responsible for his disappearance. After summoning my courage, I asked Thomas if he'd seen his nephew. Several minutes passed in silence, my husband's smirk never faltering. Enraged, I rushed around the table, grabbed his shoulders and screamed, 'Where is Johnathon?'

"And when he still refused to answer, I slapped him. Enraged, Thomas jumped from his chair. There we stood, our faces just inches apart. Oh, you should have seen the murder in his eyes! In return, he struck me brutally. It wasn't the first time he'd physically assaulted me, but this time he intended to kill. Turning on my heel, I fled the dining hall with my husband in close pursuit. As I raced toward the staircase, his diabolical laughter rang in my ears. In disbelief, I heard my husband call out that Johnathon was dead. If this was true, I'd likely be his next victim. Running for my life, I bounded up the spiraling staircase, hoping to escape into the master bedroom. And I'd almost made it to the top step, when I felt my husband's hands around my throat. In an instant, I was falling. With divine intervention, I somehow survived. When I awoke, there was nothing but pain and darkness. I tried screaming for help, but I could no longer speak.

"As you may remember from the diary, my voice box was injured when I landed on the bottom of the stairs. Just another one of Thomas's crimes. Desperate and alone, I spent hours pacing the dark attic, searching for any means of escape. Yet, just like my last imprisonment, there was no way out. Time passed excruciatingly slowly. My only human contact happened when Thomas appeared late at night outside the attic door. Without a word, he'd push a tray of table scraps across the floor, locking the dead bolt immediately behind.

"After a while, I planned for his nightly visits. Whenever I'd hear the lock rattle, I'd rush to the door. Mr. O'Shea was always too quick, slamming the door in my face. Desperate to escape, I continued pounding the walls, hoping the servants might hear me. My attempts proved fruitless. For many months, the routine repeated. Then, one stormy evening, my husband made it devastatingly clear that no one would ever find me. During a late-night visit, Thomas surprised me by entering the attic while I slept. His hair and clothes were dripping wet, as if he'd spent some time outdoors. Fearing for my life, I lay motionless as he drew closer. Silently, he moved his kerosene lantern above my shivering form. Sitting next to me on the soiled mattress, he confessed his evil deeds. I soon learned exactly what transpired after my fall. When I landed at the bottom of the staircase, my husband believed me dead. Taking my pulse, and seeing I was still alive, he carried me to an upstairs guest bedroom. For over a week I remained unconscious. When I finally awoke, Mr. O'Shea pressed a cloth of chloroform to my mouth. With the use of sedatives, he was able to keep me out of the way while he hatched his sinister plan.

"During the time I was incapacitated, he used his carpentry skills to soundproof the attic. Once construction ended, he caried me back to my prison. He'd installed a brand-new deadbolt on the door, hid the key in the master bedroom, and instructed the housekeeping staff that the room was off limits. After his confession, Thomas left me alone to contemplate my fate. Fearing I'd never be found alive, I surrendered to my melancholia. For several days, I lay listless atop my bed. Although my existence seemed futile, there was still a spark of hope remaining. Was it possible there was something I'd overlooked? Perhaps a loose floorboard or weakness in the plaster I'd missed? If I could locate some tiny opening, perhaps I might find some means of escape. Although it seemed improbable, what else could I do?

"For hours at a time, I scratched and clawed at the boarded walls, my hands becoming bruised and bloody. Sadly, my efforts were in vain, and I eventually gave up all hope. Day and evening flowed together like an endless sentence in purgatory. After weeks and months of desperate escape attempts, I prayed that death might emancipate me from my living hell. My prayers were eventually answered.

"My husband's final visit took place late in the evening. It was many hours since my last meal, and my hunger was overwhelming. After he'd tossed a moldy loaf of bread to the floor, he stood over me as I tore into it.

Once I'd finished the pathetic meal, I lay still, fearing what he might do next. Ruddy faced and reeking of bourbon, he lowered himself to the edge of the mattress. Holding the lantern to my face, he gleefully announced the news of his upcoming marriage. As thunder boomed over Monarch Cove, I wept.

There was no question in my mind Thomas intended to leave me alone to die in the attic. After a few minutes of anguished sobbing, he gathered me in his arms. It seemed at first, he'd regretted telling me, but his lustful intentions were soon revealed. Desperate to stop my husband's unwanted advances, I clawed his face, raking deep scratches into his flesh. Enraged, he grasped my right hand, pressing down until the bones splintered beneath his vice-like grip. The pain was unimaginable. After leaving me curled upon the mattress, he fled the attic. With the bolting of the door, my fate was sealed.

"Shortly after my husband's departure, I slipped into unconsciousness. When I awoke, my body was wracked in agony. Bracing my mangled hand to my chest, I moved from the bed. Remembering Thomas had brought a kerosene lamp during his visit, I prayed he'd left it behind in his haste. I felt around in the dark until I stumbled upon the lantern. But with only one usable hand, it was challenging turning on the flame. Sadly, it was no use; the oil burned while I slept. So, I waited for the dawn. With first light, I crept toward the tiny partition between the boarded windows. With joy, I viewed my portrait in the muted light.

"For the next several days, I endured the unimaginable, my only comfort was the time spent with my beloved seascape. Without food and water, it was only a matter of days before I succumbed to my terrible fate. Although the relentless solitude nearly drove me mad, it was the constant thirst which caused unbearable suffering. Near the end of my imprisonment, I could barely stand, and I began noticing tiny flickers of light haloing my final artwork. At first, I believed my eyes were deceiving me. Regardless, I focused on the illuminated canvas. Although weak in body, my mind was surprisingly alert. If I stared long enough, the ocean waves moved. Deidre shook her head. "The painting was my only source of peace in a hellish existence, and I lost myself within its magical allure. If I focused, the painted sky mirrored rosy dewdrops reflecting the vagrant beach. No longer having access to kerosene, I waited every morning for the first light of day. Half an hour of sunlight penetrated the boarded windows of the attic. I tried my best to be awake by dawn. If I overslept, I missed my opportunity to gaze at the portrait.

Twenty-three and a half hours a day I lingered in darkness. Sometimes, I'd stay up all night just to make sure I was awake in time to enjoy my beloved seaside. Over time, the imagery changed. Just minute alterations in the beginning—a different hue within the seascape, sometimes an extra cloud rising beyond the horizon. One morning, I noticed the cabin appeared closer, and a lantern flickered in the window. Was Johnathon trying to make contact? If he was, I knew I must find him! The idea kept me from giving up completely.

"Every morning when the light trickled in, I'd focus on the changing portrait, memorizing the imagery, analyzing possible alterations I'd missed. I put it all to memory. And then one day, without the help of dawn's first light, the scenery manifested in the darkness. At first, I believed my eyes were deceiving me. But soon I realized that my beloved painting was illuminating itself. And to my delight, I could see every detail. Tears of joy spilled down my hallowed cheeks as I lost myself within the sea and sky. And then, the unthinkable happened. I discovered I had the ability to change the details of the portrait with the power of my imagination.

"Of course, this took practice and patience. But what else did I have to keep me busy?" Deidre asked, with a lady-like laugh. "Every moment of the time remaining, I focused my energy on the seascape, imagining myself inside the canvas. And the outcome was delightful! With practice, I experienced the cool wind in my hair, even enjoyed the aroma of the tides. My hunger and thirst forgotten, I'd lose myself within the cresting waves and high-pitched cries of the gulls. Then, on the final day, the portrait radiated the most beautiful colors. Before I realized, I found myself inside my artwork! I could see every brushstroke, experience every burst of color released from my palette. Laughing with abandonment, I raced across the beach, my bare feet leaving footprints in the sand. Exhilarated, I moved through the valley of life and death. And to my delight, I discovered myself inside Johnathon's cabin overlooking the cliffside. When I took my final breath, a glorious radiance filled the entrance. How can I explain the experience? Words fail me. Pure joy and sublime peace welcomed me home. Moving toward the heavenly light, I called out to my beloved. But, to my dismay, Johnathon didn't answer. Hesitating, I wondered if my lover was lost in the void? If he remained on the property, would I ever see him again? Unsure, I turned away from the Divine, and wandered back towards the shadows of Monarch Cove.

"Simultaneously, I found myself beneath the spiraling staircases, gazing up at my portrait. Tears welled in my eyes; something was terribly wrong. Johnathon's painting appeared muted and grey. The vivid cerulean hue of the sea was replaced with a lack luster shade of lead. Turning away in haste, I raced through the dark corridors of Monarch Cove, crying out for my beloved. Everything I'd once known appeared lifeless and dull, even the fresh roses resting on the fireplace mantel. Servants moved about the estate oblivious to my presence. When I attempted to call out to them, my voice was clear and strong! 'Please wait! I'm right here!' I cried.

"But the housekeepers went on about their business as if I didn't exist! Without a plan, I wandered aimlessly through the manor. One fateful day, I watched Margaret, the head housekeeper, rush toward the front door. To my surprise, Thomas entered the front parlor. In his arms, he carried a young woman. The blonde-haired beauty gazed into his admiring eyes; unaware she'd married a monster.

"No longer frightened, I approached the newlyweds, demanding an explanation. And to my horror, they passed by without a second glance. In my anguish, I raced back to the seashore, once again searching for Johnathon. For days and weeks, I wandered along the cove, day turning to night. Although I no longer experienced pain, hunger, or cold, I suffered greatly. Defeated and out of options, I returned to Monarch Cove. Oh, I wasn't prepared for what greeted me. Time passed while I'd been away. The estate no longer resembled the home I'd remembered. Now a new lady of the manor resided, and she'd placed her unique touch on the mansion. Surprisingly, my portrait remained as it had before my demise. One evening, I overheard a heated argument. Thomas refused to remove Johnathon's painting, despite his second wife's protests.

"Days, weeks, and years shuffled by like a hazy dream. Servants came and went; new faces appeared. Parties were thrown in the grand ballroom; I'd watch old friends and acquaintances waltzing by, unaware of my presence. The loneliness was overwhelming, and I often cried out in my hopelessness and boredom. Other times I'd search the grounds, wandering the empty cove calling out to my beloved. But my attempts proved futile. Everything seemed hopeless until our paths crossed.

"Jade MacFie, you are my final chance. With your spiritual awareness, I was able to make contact by means of my portrait. At first, my only intention was to seek your assistance, but it soon became apparent you were in great danger yourself. The painting warned me of the Hunters' evil plans. Their leader was a vicious man, not unlike my husband. So, I pushed my own needs temporarily aside, and attempted to send you messages by means of my artwork. For you see, I am sensitive, too. It's why our paths crossed in the first place. Once you were in possession of items from Monarch Cove, I was able to make the first contact. Purchasing the antiques from *Treasures in the Attic* opened the door. I made sure my portrait ended up in your shop. It took an immense amount of concentration and energy on my part, but it was well worth the effort," Deidre said.

Jade's mouth fell open in surprise. "How incredible! I've been puzzled how the portrait ended up in my broom closet. Interestingly, the items from your estate sale were some of the original purchases for my antique store. When I discovered your painting in the broom closet, I had no idea where it came from. You see, I would have remembered ordering such a unique piece of art. The portrait's appearance coincided with the first shipment of teacups and pots from Monarch Cove. Now it finally makes sense." Jade pushed a loose curl from her eyes. "I can't thank you enough for your assistance with the Hunters. Without witnessing the changes in the painting, I'm not sure if I would have discovered Aidan's kidnappers. Your artwork provided valuable clues concerning the cult members' whereabouts. And now the portrait's led me to you. It's unbelievable. I'll do anything in my power to help you escape Thomas O'Shea."

Lady O'Shea nodded. "I sensed you were in trouble. And I'm glad I was able to assist. I only hope you can repay the favor. If I don't leave the property soon, it's only a matter of time before Thomas takes me for his own. The thought is unimaginable, an endless hell for all eternity. Our time is short. His power grows stronger by the day. I am his obsession. He continues to torment me in death as he did in life. With your psychic gifts, I pray you can help me escape his wrath. The anniversary of Johnathon's disappearance falls on Christmas Eve. Tonight, my fate hangs in the balance."

Jade moved closer, holding eye contact with the mysterious apparition.

"I'm going to help, but I'll need more information. For example, how do you use the portrait to cross over? If I have more facts, maybe we can come up with a plan."

Deidre nodded. "All I know is that the painting was the last thing I witnessed before I left the mortal world. I rejected the light of heaven to wait for Johnathon. But to my heartbreak, I became lost within a cold, grey reality. I've searched all these years in vain. And since Thomas discovered the portal, it's only a matter of time before he traps me forever," Deidre said.

"Where do we begin?" Jade asked.

Mrs. O'Shea steepled her fingers beneath her chin. "We must go back to Monarch Cove."

In silence, Deidre took Jade's hand and they walked toward the gothic estate, the wind blowing their hair back. They watched in dismay as the grey skies darkened. With Morrigan leading the way, they disappeared into the fog.

Chapter Fourteen

As Dougal growled at the portrait, Aidan's hands tightened into fists. Instinct suggested his wife was in trouble, and he suspected the painting was connected to her disappearance. From his years as a fire-fighter, he understood it was imperative to remain calm. With his terrier at his heel, he took a quick walk around the cottage, calling out his wife's name. Noticing Morrigan missing from her perch turned his blood cold. Jade wouldn't take Morrigan and leave Dougal behind.

A tapping at the door drove him from his thoughts. He bolted across the room, blindly hoping his wife would be on the other side. When he saw the face of Madame Garnier, his heart sank. Her dark eyes burned with urgency.

"Mr. MacFie, Jade is in great danger."

Aidan ushered the elderly woman inside and closed the door.

"What do you know? Please, tell me everything."

"I received a startling vision this evening," she said, walking toward the fireplace, grimacing at the changes of the altered portrait.

"This is what I feared. My visions are never wrong. Oh, I wish they were sometimes," Madame Garnier said, shaking her lace covered head.

"I don't understand. What's happened to Jade?"

"She's moved into the veil. Prepare yourself. A battle of good and evil is upon us." The psychic-medium moved toward the couch, sucking in her breath when she spotted the walking stick propped against the side.

"What is that?" Aidan asked.

The elderly woman made the sign of the cross.

"Thomas O'Shea was in your cottage. My greatest fear has come to fruition. There is no time to spare. We must leave for Monarch Cove before it's too late!"

Without another word, Aidan fetched Dougal's leash, the puppy carrier, an umbrella, and his car keys before escorting the psychic-medium to his SUV.

While hail peppered the windshield, Aidan turned to Madame Garnier. "Please, just explain what I must do to save my wife."

"Young man, I'll tell you everything I can, but steel yourself. It's imperative you keep your faith close to your heart. Please listen carefully. When we face the Evil One, time will be of the essence."

Aidan nodded soberly, listening quietly as Madame Garnier explained her recent vision. His stomach clenched as he tried to mentally prepare for the upcoming battle. With years of experience fighting fires, and recently Hunters, this new threat seemed unfathomable. How could he combat something unholy? An entity, not of this world? The idea filled him with dread, but he realized he'd do everything in his power to save his beloved. His chiseled jaw clenched as lightning flashed in the distance. The storm had arrived.

Chapter Fifteen

MOMENTS BEFORE AIDAN MACFIE ENTERED THE COTTAGE, THOMAS O'Shea was watching his former wife and companion disappear through the portrait. Seething with rage, he gazed around the living room, looking for something to release his anger upon. The corners of his mouth lifted when he noticed the Scottish Terrier snapping at his feet. Reaching out a claw-like hand toward its wiry neck, the ghostly apparition was instantly repelled by an invisible forcefield. Astounded, he realized Deidre had used her powers to protect the mutt.

Disappointed he couldn't kill the nuisance, he turned his attention to the portrait above the fireplace. He'd intended to tear the animal limb from limb for the women's disobedience. No matter, he thought, trying to refocus his energy. He'd aim his fury toward the lasses instead. Oh, he had such plans for them. An eternity of punishment would be unleashed. Closing his eyes, he imagined his old estate. Simultaneously, he found himself inside the parlor of Monarch Cove, gazing up at the portrait of Lady Deidre O'Shea. He grinned, sensing the women nearby. There was no rush to fish them out just yet; there was nowhere to run. Feeling a rush of contentment, he studied the painting resting between the spiraling staircases.

Over the years, he'd grown to despise his former wife with all of heart and soul. He blamed her for binding him to the cursed property. If Deidre believed she could escape him in the afterlife, she was sadly mistaken.

Through the years she'd eluded him, always disappearing just moments before he could lay hands on her. And Thomas remembered the way she tormented him after her death, making herself known in every dark recess of Monarch Cove. His servants thought him mad when he'd scream out his wrath at the portrait. They couldn't see her, but she was always there just out of reach, taunting. His rage burned brightly over the decades. He crossed his arms and sighed, thinking back through the years. Their future could have been one filled with bliss and enchantment. If she'd only submitted herself to him body and soul, things would have turned out quite differently. In the beginning of their marriage, Thomas enjoyed his young wife. Yet, he had a nagging suspicion her feelings were not mutual.

Despite her reserved demeanor, he tried enticing her with expensive presents, even gifted her a beautiful art studio. What did she do in return? She repaid him by flaunting herself around Carmel like a common harlot, enticing all kinds of riffraff by the seaside. He had no choice but to put the lass in her place, believing solitary confinement in the attic would put an end to her whorish ways. But when opportunity arose, she took up with his nephew, sealing both their fates. It seems like only yesterday he'd discovered Johnathon alone in his cabin, packing his meager possessions, preparing to run off with Deidre like a thief in the night. His brother's son believed himself clever, but Thomas had eyes on him the entire time. It wasn't difficult. Paying off a servant here and there confirmed all his suspicions, including their plans to flee to Ireland together.

Mr. O'Shea grinned up at the portrait, remembering the night he'd barged into his nephew's cabin. Despite the boy's shock of being confronted by his uncle, he readily confessed his love for Deidre.

"What a fool he was, just like his father before him," Thomas O'Shea whispered between the spiraling staircases, pacing in circles. He pointed a claw-like hand toward the portrait, flashing his eerie grin.

"My dearest, Deidre. Imagine my amusement when your beloved Johnathon threatened to leave by force if I didn't move out of his way. Must have believed he could overpower me on account of his youth. Ha! The lad was sadly mistaken. My pathetic nephew didn't realize I had a weapon behind my back the entire time we were speaking," he shouted at the portrait. "Oh, Mrs. O'Shea, your lover's skull splintered beneath the blow of my blackjack like a ripe pumpkin! How I roared with laughter, watching him writhing on the floor, trying in vain to rise. If only you could have witnessed your knight in shining armor crawling toward the doorway like a beaten mongrel. But I wasn't finished with him just yet. No. When he finally reached the barrier, I kicked him vigorously in the ribs. Ah, so much blood poured from his gaping mouth! Yet, nothing seemed to stop the lad. It was only when I stomped upon his splayed hands that he surrendered. I can still recall the sound of his bones splintering beneath my heal and his anguished screams. 'No more painting for you, lad,' I cried!'

"Well, nearly an hour passed, and I realized our lovely guests would be arriving for the Christmas Eve party. So, it was time to finish the job. Darlin', do you know your lover repeatedly called out your name in his final moments? In fact, his last words were, 'I love you, Deidre!' Pathetic. Of course, you didn't hear him. You were upstairs getting ready for the portrait unveiling. In the dim light of twilight, I tightened my hands around his throat, watching with satisfaction the life fade from his eyes. Once he breathed his last, I dragged his limp body toward the cliffside overlooking the balmy sea. I tossed him to the tides like the garbage he was. I'm certain his corpse made for a lovely supper for the sharks and sea life in the cove. Well, no one discovered him. Perhaps that's why his spirit never appeared inside Monarch Cove. Quite puzzling. I've contemplated this fact many times over the years. After much consideration, I've surmised that a soul must perish within the walls of our cursed estate in order to stay on in the afterlife. No matter. Your beloved Johnathon is gone forever. I want you to remember that while we spend our eternity together. It was all for nothing, your little fling.

"Oh, how I wish he would appear again, though. I'd love another chance to torture the scoundrel. No matter: there will be many opportunities to punish you instead. My mistake was being too lenient during our marriage. I've learned my lesson, dear one. If you believed rotting away in the attic was hell, just wait for what I have in store. Tonight, will be the beginning of your proper training as my wife. You will learn the art of obedience. And your mortal companion will make a lovely pupil as well. Yes, this Christmas Eve we will renew our vows. It will be a night to remember. Get ready, lasses. It's almost time to celebrate!"

WHILE THOMAS RAGED, THUNDER BOOMED ABOVE THE MANSION'S STEEPLY pitched gables. Escaping the torrential storm sweeping over the gothic manor, Deidre and Jade entered the haunted halls of Monarch Cove. Once inside the parlor, they crept across polished marble floors. In the cover of darkness, the women watched in horror as the madman roared with laughter. Deidre's hands clenched overhearing Thomas O'Shea's confession. As she learned the fate of her beloved, her hazel eyes welled with tears. Although she had suspected her husband of murdering Johnathon, she now knew it to be a fact. And the painful way in which he died nearly brought her to her knees in anguish.

Jade took Deidre's hand, eyes full of sympathy.

"Lady O'Shea, he's no longer suffering. Since Johnathon's absent from the property, he must have moved on to the other side. And that is where you must go."

"But how will I find the light again? It vanished over a century ago. And what if you're wrong? I can't bear the thought of losing my beloved for all eternity. Now that I know the truth of Thomas's crime, I refuse to wait another moment to confront him. My husband will pay for taking the life of his nephew. If it's the last thing I do, I will have my revenge!"

With lantern in hand, Mrs. O'Shea pushed past Jade.

"Deidre, no!" Jade whispered, trying to stop her. Within seconds, Thomas and Deidre were face-to-face beneath the portrait.

Jade watched in horror as the scene unfolded.

Mr. O'Shea flashed a satisfied smile. "Finally, you've come back, darlin'. Did you miss me?"

Without a second thought, Jade moved from the shadows. Even without a weapon or source of protection, she refused to let Deidre face the monster alone. After all, Mrs. O'Shea had saved her numerous times by means of her portrait, and she intended to return the favor.

Jade felt her stomach clench as Thomas O'Shea's muddy eyes bore into her.

"Oh, what a sweet young lass. You could have saved yourself, but here you are defending my infamous wife. I'm not sure if you're impossibly brave or just a simple fool. No matter. You've made your choice and will pay a hefty price for your impertinence. Prepare yourself. Once you perish within the halls of Monarch Cove, your soul will be bound to the estate for all eternity. And I must say, it will be delightful enjoying both your body and soul," Thomas said, biting his bottom lip. "Oh, this will indeed be a night to remember!"

Jade bowed her head and silently prayed. *Please stand by my side, mom and gram. I need your help tonight.*

෮෫෯

WHILE THOMAS O'SHEA THREATENED JADE, MADAME GARNIER AND Aidan entered the haunted mansion by the front door.

Madame Garnier realized Aidan was preparing to confront the demon, so she beckoned him to stop. Impatient, he hesitated only when the psychic stepped out in front of him, blocking his way.

"Aidan, your wife is already in the presence of the Dark One. Before saving her, we must prepare for an exorcism. Do you hear the voices coming from the parlor?" As she said this, he turned his head, overhearing maniacal laughter from the next room.

Aidan nodded, clenching his fists in agitation.

"Before you rush the scene, it's important we open a window first. Once this is done, I'll begin the cleansing ritual."

"Why must we open a window?" Aidan asked, his brow furrowing.

"The window will provide an exit for the evil spirt to leave our earthly realm. The demon must be banished. Make sense?"

Aidan nodded, while escorting Madame Garnier through the dark corridor.

Silently, they moved across the parlor toward the spiraling staircases. Moments later, they were in earshot of Thomas O'Shea and the women. The psychic pointed her gloved hand toward the bay window in the back of the room.

Without a word, Aidan moved toward the lace-covered glass. As quietly as possible, he lifted the sill. Instantly, a blast of icy rain peppered his face. Standing within the shadows, he waited for a confrontation. To his surprise, the disruption went unnoticed.

Madame Garnier patted Aidan's bicep and whispered, "Excellent, young man. They don't seem aware of our presence just yet. But they will. Once I address the demon, you may go to your wife. Please wait for my cue."

"I'll try my best, but I can't promise. I'm not standing by if Jade's life is in danger."

"I understand your concern. Please just give me a few minutes to begin. If you feel you must, then help her."

Aidan touched Madame Garnier on the small of her back, leading her toward the sound of eerie laughter. With Bible and rosary in hand, the psychic-medium followed the firefighter into battle.

⁊⁊⁊

WHEN JADE LIFTED HER HEAD, SHE HEARD FOOTSTEPS BEHIND HER. Turning, she watched in astonishment as Aidan and Madame Garnier entered the room.

"Aidan?" Jade whispered, wondering why he lingered in the doorway.

Madame Garnier locked eyes with Thomas O'Shea. Steadfast, she readied herself to address the apparition. Before she could utter a word, the entity's eyes turned a startling shade of citrine yellow, and his grotesquely long arms raised toward the ceiling. To her dismay, the wallpaper blackened and pealed, sloughing onto the ground in smoldering heaps. The pungent aroma of sulfur filled the space. As she feared, the presence was powerful, able to manipulate its surroundings with ease. Banishing the creature was going to take all her powers and decades of experience.

"You think you can stop me, old woman? You will die before the sun rises on Christmas morning!"

Jade's brow raised, gazing into her husband's loving eyes from the other side of the room. "How did you find us?"

"I promised I'd never let anything happen to you, lass," Aidan said.

Thomas O'Shea turned toward Jade with a smirk. "Don't think your man can protect you. Say your goodbyes for your life was forfeited the moment you assisted Deidre. I hope you remember this as we go forward. Prepare for a lifetime of obedience and servitude. I look forward to devouring your body and soul!"

"Go to hell, ye filthy bastard!" Aidan yelled, rushing forward.

"I'm already in hell, mortal. And your lovely lady will be joining me shortly." As he said this, Jade levitated toward the ceiling. With legs and arms akimbo, she appeared to be taking flight.

"Jade!" Aidan yelled, attempting to grab her legs as she ascended. Infuriated, he watched helplessly as she rose toward the stained-glass windows. A streak of lighting illuminated the aperture, sending a kaleidoscope of color throughout the room.

"What's happening?" Jade screamed, struggling with the invisible force controlling her body.

Madame Garnier moved forward, locking eyes with her friend. "Be brave, child! Summon your angels and concentrate. We are here with you."

Madame Garnier glanced over at Aidan and Deidre.

"There is no time to lose. Take my hand and pray the Lord's Prayer!"

Aidan's jaw clenched as he took the psychic's hand. Deidre moved closer, and they created a prayer circle beneath Jade's floating body.

Madame Garnier opened her Bible.

"Let us begin.

> *Our Father who art in heaven,*
> *Hallowed be thy name*
> *Thy kingdom come*
> *Thy will be done*
> *On earth as it is in heaven*
> *Give us this day our daily bread*
> *And forgive us our trespasses*
> *As we forgive those who trespass against us*
> *And lead us not into temptation*
> *But deliver us from evil*
> *For thine is the kingdom and the power, and the*
>   *glory*
> *Forever and ever*
> *Amen."*

While the holy words were spoken, a hot wind swirled throughout the room, bringing with it the aroma of sulfur and decay. Thomas O'Shea's face elongated and blistered until the flesh sloughed off into meaty chunks. By the glow of Deidre's kerosene lamp, reptilian scales replaced his human flesh. Within seconds, needle-sharp fangs dropped from its gaping maw, and an ebony tongue flickered in the soft light. Despite his animalistic appearance, the demon managed to speak in a deep, guttural tone.

"You think your prayers will save you? The lasses belong to me, and

I'm looking forward to breaking in my new wife." As he pointed razor-sharp talons, Jade fell toward the marble stonework.

"Jade!" Aidan yelled, rushing toward his wife.

In that moment, Jade pictured her mother's face. Simultaneously, she experienced the sensation of an invisible embrace. Just inches from crashing to the floor, she stopped mid-air before being gently lowered to the ground. There was no doubt in her mind that her ancestors' divine intervention prevented her from falling to her death. Stunned, she watched her husband race to her side. Gathering her into his powerful arms, he glared at the demonic apparition across the room.

"Ye foul bastard! You'll pay for laying hands on my wife!"

As soon as the words left his mouth, Jade flew backward into the arms of what was once Thomas O'Shea. Within seconds, the lizard-like creature clutched Jade against his scaly chest.

As Aidan took a step forward, he was immediately propelled across the room, crashing against the scorched wallpaper below Deidre O'Shea's fallen portrait. After hitting the ground, he laid motionless.

"Aidan!" Jade screamed, trying to escape the demon's powerful hold. His reptilian body wreaked of decay, and her stomach churned in response to the putrid odor. Holding her tightly, the creature roared with laughter.

"You think your god will protect you? You're wrong! The lasses belong to me. I've grown tired of this crone and her ridiculous rituals," he said, turning his gaze on Madame Garnier. "I'd planned to kill you quickly, old woman, but I've changed my mind. Prepare to suffer a gruesome and agonizing death. Before it's over, you'll be begging me to put you out of your misery."

Madame Garnier gripped her Bible, ebony eyes fixed on the demon. Grasping her crucifix, she repeated in a strong, steady voice, "Thomas O'Shea, In the name of Jesus Christ, I banish you from this house!"

His smirk faded when he realized the psychic's true power. In response, Jade made the sign of the cross and repeated the psychic's command.

"In the name of Jesus Christ, we banish you from this house!" For a moment, Jade felt the entity's grip weaken. Taking advantage of the situation, she pulled away from its clutches and raced toward her fallen husband.

As her arms encircled Aidan, a terrible splintering sound echoed above. Within seconds, the stained-glass aperture shattered, sending colorful shards in every direction. Jade covered her husband's body with her own, while Madame Garnier clutched her Bible close to her bosom.

After summoning her remaining faith, Deidre O'Shea stretched nimble fingers toward the raining kaleidoscope and shouted, "In the name of all that is holy, protect my friends from the Dark One's wrath! In Jesus' name, we pray."

After several moments of ear-splitting chaos and falling debris, the group slowly raised themselves from the floor. To their astonishment, the glass particles were gathered in spherical piles against the back wall. Turning toward Deidre in quiet awe, the friends realized how close they'd come to losing their mortal lives. With divine faith, Mrs. O'Shea made sure they remained unharmed.

Aidan's ocean-blue eyes slowly opened as Jade cradled his head in her lap. After getting back on their feet, the group gathered beneath the protection of the gothic archway. Despite no one being seriously injured, the tempest's formidable rain and wind swept throughout the room, sending lamps and framed photographs to the floor. The friends watched the lizard-like demon levitate between the spiraling staircases. When he reached the damaged ceiling, he grabbed the razor-sharp edges in order to prevent being pulled into the eye of the storm. As his body twisted and turned, blood flowed from his bleeding talons. The sound of thunder boomed overhead as the inky darkness gave way to swirling scarlet rays. Jade put her hand to her mouth, holding her breath. Madame Garnier made the sign of the cross as the group watched legions of demonic spirits appear within the garnet-colored vortex. Within seconds, the terrifying apparitions surrounded Thomas O'Shea, their claw-like hands raking and gashing his writhing body.

"No!" the creature screamed as his scaly flesh melted from his face, revealing pulsing capillaries and oozing sores. Just before he was pulled into the portal, Mr. O'Shea glared down at his former wife.

"I'll never leave this house, Deidre! Our souls are bound together for all eternity. If I'm headed to hell, so are you!"

The Lady in Grey stood her ground and considered the creature's words.

"Thomas, you were merciless in both life and death, but you no longer hold power over me. I forgive you. You are no longer bound to this place and time. Pray forgiveness from our Holy Father. It's never too late to be saved."

For a moment, the demon's citrine eyes filled with tears. Seemingly stunned by Deidre's compassion, he regarded her with disbelief. While Thomas hovered between the veils of good and evil, a radiant prism of light appeared between the spiraling staircases. Near the blackened wall where Lady O'Shea's portrait once hung, Johnathon O'Shea transfigured into the world of the living. When Thomas laid eyes on his nephew, his eyes darkened with rage.

"I'll never accept your mercy, whore. And don't think you're going to have your happy ever after with my bastard nephew."

Breaking free from the legions of unholy spirits, he descended. As his feet struck the marble floor, he kicked over Deidre's discarded lamp. When his oozing flesh connected with the spilled kerosene, his body immediately burst into flames. Twisting, and turning in the wind, Deidre watched in horror as his body melted to the bone.

Despite the terrorizing scene, Madame Garnier wasted no time in reacting to the situation.

"In the name of Jesus Christ, leave this house!"

A choral of demonic voices rose in answer as the remains of Thomas O'Shea propelled through the open window in the back of the room. Once his ashes disappeared into the stormy night, Aidan limped toward the fluttering curtains and locked the window. Jade rushed to her husband and flung her arms around him.

"Are you alright, love?"

Aidan offered his lopsided smile. "I'll live. Wouldn't mind a wee dram of whiskey tonight, though. Might be a bit sore tomorrow, but nothing serious." He chuckled, gazing down at Jade's concerned face. "Don't worry. Not the first time I've been thrown into a wall or knocked unconscious, for that matter."

Jade's eyebrows rose in question.

"Life of a fireman, darlin'. I'll be just fine."

"Oh, right," she said, brushing the damp curls from his eyes. Just as the couple was beginning to relax, their attention was diverted by the bright spectrum of light radiating by the fallen portrait. Within the vivid display, a young gentleman's silhouette appeared. Deidre gasped in astonishment when she recognized the handsome youth. Rushing into his arms, she felt her lover's hands encircle her petite waist. She blinked in astonishment, tears of joy running down her pale face.

"Johnathon, you came back! I've been waiting for so long."

"Oh, how I've missed my beautiful lass!" he said, gathering her to his brawny chest. Johnathon lifted Deidre into his powerful arms as if she weighed nothing. "God, you're a lovely sight. Deidre, my love, are you ready to go home?" he asked, raising her hand to his lips.

With splayed fingers, she cupped the broad nape of her lover's neck. "I've been waiting for over a century. Please!"

Beaming into her hazel eyes, Johnathon leaned closer. "I tried to come back for you many years ago, but you left before my arrival. This time, I made sure I wouldn't miss ye. We've been apart far too long. But I promise with all my heart and soul, we'll make up for time lost. From this day forward, we'll never be apart. I'm looking forward to spending an eternity loving my beautiful lass."

After sharing a passionate kiss, Deidre snuggled against Johnathon. Before disappearing into the heavenly light, Lady O'Shea glanced over her shoulder and smiled.

"My dear friends, I'm forever grateful for your compassion. I've prayed for many years to be reunited with my beloved. Go forward and have a blessed life. And Jade, your ancestors' presence, shines brightly through the veil. Oh, they love you so, Lady MacFie."

As the couple moved forward into the sublime light, the sound of violins surrounded them. Johnathon beamed down at Deidre, love radiating in his whisky-brown eyes. At peace in his loving arms, The Grey Lady of Monarch Cove crossed into the heavenly veil.

⊗⚶⊗

MADAME GARNIER PLACED HER GLOVED HANDS OVER HER HEART AND smiled. "Mademoiselle, your gift is extraordinary. Congratulations on helping your first soul cross the veil. If I were to bet, I think your services will be called on again. But have no fear, it will always be your choice to help those in need."

Jade nodded, suddenly feeling there was someone else who required her assistance.

"Thank you, but I'm sensing we may not have to wait very long. There is one more ghostly presence residing in Monarch Cove."

Madame Garnier nodded. "I wondered if you might sense it, too. Very good. Please take the lead."

Jade took a breath, summoning her courage.

"Mrs. Dunsmuir, are you here?" Jade called out.

For several minutes, there was only the sound of the wind and falling rain. As lightning flashed above the shattered stained-glass aperture, the room filled with the scent of eucalyptus and stale tobacco. Wearing her vivid canary yellow pantsuit, Abby Dunsmuir stood beneath the spiraling staircases. With cigarette in hand, she surveyed the group.

"Oh, Mrs. MacFie! I had the feeling you'd be back. Second thoughts on purchasing Monarch Cove?" she asked, her pale blue eyes sparkling in the dim light.

Jade shook her head and offered a gentle smile.

"Mrs. Dunsmuir, it's your time to cross over," Jade said as a beam of colorful light manifested behind the elderly realtor.

The ghostly figure blinked in confusion, slowly turning toward the radiant spectrum.

"You want me to leave Monarch Cove? What a strange notion."

"Yes, it's time."

Abby studied the heavenly hues twinkling between the staircases.

"Such lovely colors, but I just don't think I'm ready to vacate just yet."

Jade held her breath, trying to decide how to persuade the lost soul into the light when a high-pitched barking echoed from the bright tunnel. Abby Dunsmuir's hand went to her heart as she watched her beloved dog emerge from the veil. Rainbow prisms haloed the puppy's petite silhouette.

Abby's pale eyes widened as the cinnamon-colored dachshund jumped into her loving arms.

"Daisy? Oh, my beautiful girl! I've missed you so!" Abby laughed as the happy pup smothered her with wet kisses. Hugging her pet tightly, she grinned, tears streaking down her wrinkled face.

"How can I ever thank you?" she asked, holding the dog to her frail chest. Within moments, a glorious halo enveloped the pair. As the spirits departed, the room filled with the scent of rose petals.

Madame Garnier smiled proudly, placing her hand on Jade's shoulder.

"Very good, mademoiselle. You've done well. I think it's best we leave now. Our work is done," she said, glancing toward Jade's abdomen. "You should rest when you get home. Many exciting surprises await you and your handsome husband."

Jade nodded slowly, sensing something just out of reach.

Aidan escorted Jade and Madame Garnier outside to the SUV. The psychic-medium insisted Jade take the front seat, choosing to sit in the back with Dougal, Morrigan, and the puppy carrier. Distracted, Jade failed to notice the new occupant in the backseat. As they headed home, Jade struggled to keep her eyes open. Once they reached Madame Garnier's modest bungalow, Aidan opened an umbrella and waited for the women to say their goodbyes. As Madame Garnier turned to leave, she locked eyes with Jade. "Well, I believe your charming husband will be receiving a lovely Christmas surprise. God bless you both," she said, squeezing Jade's hand.

Aidan's brow rose in question. Holding his umbrella over the elderly woman, he led her to her front door. In the dim light, her cats encircled her with their high-pitched greeting.

"My precious babies! I have extra treats and toys ready for our Christmas celebration! Pyewacket, you were of great help tonight." She lifted her familiar into her arms, kissing the back of his dark head. After thanking Aidan, she waved goodbye, eager to share some holiday cheer with her beloved entourage. Once Madame Garnier was safely inside, Aidan returned to the SUV, and gathered Jade in his arms.

"What do you suppose Madame Garnier was talking about? Is there a surprise I should know about?" he asked.

Jade shrugged her shoulders. "Your guess is as good as mine," she said, trying to rein in her growing excitement. Is my life about to change in an instant? And if so, would Aidan be happy about the news?

"Darling, I don't know what would have happened if you hadn't arrived on time. Thank God; you found us. I think we might finally have things back to normal…" Jade said, stopping mid-sentence.

A high-pitched whimper from the backseat caused her to jump in her seat.

"What on earth is that noise?" she asked, noticing Dougal sitting quietly beside her.

Aidan chuckled and reached for the carrier. "I was wondering when you'd notice, lass. One of your Christmas presents is in the back seat. Hope you like it."

With a lopsided grin, he gently placed the wiggling puppy onto Jade's lap. When his wife's grey eyes filled with tears, he reached for her hand.

"Aidan, she's absolutely gorgeous!"

"Glad you approve, darlin'. You'd mentioned owning a poodle when you were young. Figured a wee pup might bring a smile to your lovely face."

"Oh, she's absolutely perfect!"

As the puppy smothered her new owner with kisses, Dougal curled onto Jade's lap.

"You're a good boy, too!" The terrier's stubby tail wiggled as he let out a high-pitched bark.

"Looks like you're a big brother, Dougal," Aidan said.

Morrigan cawed from the back seat.

"And you're a big sister!" Jade said.

"Wow, it's been a wild Christmas Eve, lass. Not quite how I imagined spending it with my new bride."

"Yes, tonight was incredible. So relieved Deidre and Abby were able to cross over into the light. I'm so happy for them."

"Aye, you're a brave one. That was a scary situation, but ye didn't hesitate to stand up against that horrible creature and assist the ladies. Quite remarkable. I'm proud of you, love."

Jade put her hand to her head as a wave of fatigue rushed over her. The bizarre evening was catching up with her.

"Well, I didn't feel very brave. Quite terrified, in fact," Jade said.

"You hid your feelings well, darlin'. You were a natural. Just glad all of this is behind us. I say we curl up by the fireplace tonight and enjoy some peace and quiet," Aidan said, giving his wife an admiring smile. "I forgot to mention, that's a lovely robe you're wearing. Haven't seen it before."

"Thank you. Was planning to surprise my hubby with a little Christmas cheer tonight. That is, until things went off the rails," she said, blushing.

"Sound like the perfect Christmas present!" Aidan said, glancing down at his wife's hour-glass figure. "Aye, we still have time, if you're not too tired."

Jade stifled a yawn. "I think I can rally for my handsome husband. Just need to freshen up a bit."

"Sounds good." Aidan said, taking his wife's hand as he drove down the stormy highway.

Jade relaxed against the passenger seat as the heater warmed her chilled body. Just as she was beginning to doze, she heard her husband parking the SUV onto the cobblestone driveway. With Morrigan perched on her shoulder, Aidan helped bring the rest of their pets inside the cottage. After setting the alarm, he turned to his wife. "I'll feed the animals if you want to freshen up. Take your time. I'll put some wood on the fire and pour us some wine."

Jade nodded, wondering if wine would even be an option tonight. Holding her breath, she made her way to the bathroom. Catching her reflection in the mirror, she exhaled. Despite the recent scare, her cheeks were flushed, and her eyes sparkled in the dim light.

"This is crazy," she whispered to herself, reaching for the pregnancy test beneath the sink.

A few minutes later, Jade entered the living room with her hands behind her back. Aidan sat on the couch, both dogs asleep on his lap.

"Aww, there's my bonnie bride." Aidan's eyes filled with desire, admiring his wife's silky lingerie.

Jade feigned a smile, glancing at the crystal flute in her husband's hand.

"It's my turn to give you your gift; I hope you like it."

"What's not to like?" he said, the corners of his mouth lifting. When Jade didn't take her glass, he set both drinks on the table, and folded his hands over his chest. "Your lacy garb is fetching, darlin'. Looking forward to peeking underneath," he said with a wink.

Her heart thrummed as she took her seat next to him. Releasing a pent-up breath, she handed her husband the pregnancy test.

For a moment, he just stared at the bright blue plus sign.

Jade's heart raced, wondering what he was thinking. Then, his face lit up and he offered his familiar lop-sided grin.

Gently setting the test down on the table, he gathered Jade into his powerful embrace.

"You're with child, love?" he whispered in her ear, tears brimming in his aqua-marine eyes.

"I am. Hope that's okay?"

"Okay? My God, lass! This is the most incredible gift ye could give me!" He lifted her onto his lap, kissing her passionately in front of the fire.

For several moments, they held each other, listening to the crackling logs.

Aidan's eyes filled with concern, studying his wife in the firelit room.

"Are you okay, darlin'? My God, ye could have been hurt tonight!" he said, running his large hand over her silk clad belly.

Jade laughed, shaking her head. "Don't worry, I'm perfectly fine. Just a bit tired. Was just worried what you'd think about all this. I know we haven't really planned or even discussed having a family. After all, we've only been married a few weeks..."

He beamed down at her concerned face before kissing her forehead.

"You're wondering what I think?" His dimples deepened while the corners of his mouth lifted. "Why, ye made me the happiest man on earth. Been thinking about the possibility for some time, but was afraid to ask your thoughts on the matter." Aidan's face grew serious as he considered Jade. "Does it bother you that our bairn might be carrying the hybrid selkie gene?"

Jade slid the back of her hand over Aidan's cheek, relishing the feel of his afternoon shadow.

"Not at all! It's a bit of a surprise, but I'm excited. And this might sound silly, but I'm already falling in love with our little...bairn."

Aidan grinned, gazing down at his wife's flushed face.

"Aye, it's a beautiful thing! Just imagine; we're going to have our own family. Such a blessing."

Gathering his blushing bride in his arms, he turned to leave for their bedroom. Just as Aidan passed by the fireplace, Morrigan the Raven landed on the hearth. Cawing and flapping, the bird's ivory wings grazed their Christmas stockings. Once Morrigan perched, Jade cried out in surprise.

"Are you alright, love?" he asked, eyes full of worry.

"Yes, but look at the painting, Aidan!" When she said this, her husband gazed up at the phantom portrait. No longer any trace of the mysterious grey lady or Scottish laird remained. In their absence, a painted version of Aidan and Jade embraced in front of the sea's cresting waves. Between the loving couple sat a dark-haired toddler playing in the sand. With the back to the viewer, the gender was difficult to determine. One thing was evident, and that was the love shared between the beautiful family.

Tears of joy streaked down Jade's face. "I think everything is finally going to be alright," she said, catching her breath.

Aidan kissed the back of his wife's hand, holding her close.

"Merry Christmas, Lady MacFie."

"Merry Christmas, Laird MacFie," Jade said, grinning up into her husband's loving eyes.

As the storm raged over their beachfront cottage, Aidan carried his young wife to bed. With Christmas morning fresh on the horizon, the newlyweds celebrated the continuation of the MacFie Legacy.

Don't miss out on your next favorite book!

Join the Satin Romance mailing list
www.satinromance.com/mail.html

THANK YOU FOR READING

❦

Did you enjoy this book?

We invite you to leave a review at your favorite book site, such as
Goodreads, Amazon, Barnes & Noble, etc.

DID YOU KNOW THAT LEAVING A REVIEW...

- Helps other readers find books they may enjoy.
- Gives you a chance to let your voice be heard.
- Gives authors recognition for their hard work.
- Doesn't have to be long. A sentence or two about why you liked the book will do.

About the Author

AnneMarie Dapp is a graduate of San Francisco State University, where she studied Studio Arts and Art History. She lives and writes on Château Autumn Lady, her and her husband Dale's vegetarian farm, nestled within the magical Sierra Nevada Mountain Range of Northern California.

https://sockmonkey.live

facebook.com/AnneMarieDapp68

twitter.com/AnneMarieDapp

instagram.com/annemariedapp

pinterest.com/duckmomma1

Also by AnneMarie Dapp
WITH SATIN ROMANCE

White Raven Series

Prairie Ghosts

The Phantom Portrait

Selkies of Scotland

The Grey Lady of Monarch Cove

www.ingramcontent.com/pod-product-compliance
Lightning Source LLC
Chambersburg PA
CBHW021018180626
46814CB00003B/1336